$22.95

TEENS&
Relationships

ROGER E. HERNÁNDEZ

THE GALLUP YOUTH SURVEY:

MAJOR ISSUES AND TRENDS

TEENS & Relationships

ROGER E. HERNÁNDEZ

Produced by OTTN Publishing, Stockton, New Jersey

Mason Crest Publishers
370 Reed Road
Broomall, PA 19008
www.masoncrest.com

First printing

1 3 5 7 9 8 6 4 2

Library of Congress Cataloging-in-Publication Data

Hernández, Roger E.
  Teens and relationships / Roger E. Hernández.
    p. cm. — (The Gallup Youth Survey, major issues and trends)
  Includes bibliographical references and index.
  ISBN 1-59084-875-6
  1. Interpersonal relations in adolescence—United States—Juvenile literature.
  I. Title. II. Series.
  BF724.3.I58H46 2005
  158.2'0835—dc22
                      2004013751

Contents

Introduction

By George Gallup

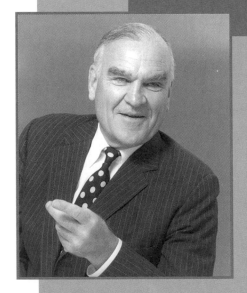

As the United States moves into the new century, there is a vital need for insight into what it means to be a young person in America. Today's teenagers—the so-called "Y Generation"—will be the leaders and shapers of the 21st century. The future direction of the United States is being determined now in their hearts and minds and actions. Yet how much do we as a society know about this important segment of the U.S. populace who have the potential to lift our nation to new levels of achievement and social health?

The nation's teen population will top 30 million by the year 2006, the highest number since 1975. Most of these teens will grow up to be responsible citizens and leaders. But some youths face very long odds against reaching adulthood physically safe, behaviorally sound, and economically self-supporting. The challenges presented to society by the less fortunate youth are enormous. To help meet these challenges it is essential to have an accurate picture of the present status of teenagers.

The Gallup Youth Survey—the oldest continuing survey of teenagers—exists to help society meet its responsibility to youth, as well as to inform and guide our leaders by probing the social and economic attitudes and behaviors of young people. With theories abounding about the views, lifestyles, and values of adolescents, the Gallup Youth Survey, through regular scientific measurements of teens themselves, serves as a sort of reality check.

We need to hear more clearly the voices of young people, and to help them better articulate their fears and their hopes. Our youth have much to share with their elders—is the older generation really listening? Is it carefully monitoring the hopes and fears of teenagers today? Failure to do so could result in severe social consequences.

Surveys reveal that the image of teens in the United States today is a negative one. Teens are frequently maligned, misunderstood, or simply ignored by their elders. Yet two decades of the Gallup Youth Survey have provided ample evidence of the very special qualities of the nation's youngsters. In fact, if our society is less racist, less sexist, less polluted, and more peace loving, we can in considerable measure thank our young people, who have been on the leading edge on these issues.

And the younger generation is not geared to greed: survey after survey has shown that teens have a keen interest in helping those people, especially in their own communities, who are less fortunate than themselves

Young people tell the Gallup Youth Survey that they are enthusiastic about helping others, and are willing to work for world peace and a healthy world. They feel positive about their schools and even more positive about their teachers. A large majority of American teenagers report that they are happy and excited about the future, feel very close to their families, are likely to marry, want to have children, are satisfied with their personal lives, and desire to reach the top of their chosen careers.

But young adults face many threats, so parents, guardians, and concerned adults must commit themselves to do everything possible to help tomorrow's parents, citizens, and leaders avoid or overcome risky behaviors so that they can move into the future with greater hope and understanding.

The Gallup Organization and the Gallup Youth Survey are enthusiastic about this partnership with Mason Crest Publishers. Through carefully and clearly written books on a variety of vital topics dealing with teens, Gallup Youth Survey statistics are presented in a way that gives new depth and meaning to the data. The focus of these books is a practical one—to provide readers with the statistics and solid information that they need to understand and to deal with each important topic.

* * *

Relationships—with one's parents, friends, romantic partners, and others—largely define who a person is and what that person is likely to become. Drawing upon surveys and other information, the author of this book examines the relationship between teens and their parents, as well as the impact of divorce and single-parent homes. He devotes a chapter to cliques, and cites information that reveals both the positive and negative impact of such groups in the lives of teenagers. While cliques provide emotional support and social skills and help teens gain an identity, there is a darker side to such groups—they contribute to unruly behavior in schools, and to a climate of fear among students for their physical safety.

"Peer pressure," named by teens as one of the biggest problems they face, is often stronger than the pressure exerted by parents, and contributes to risky behavior such as alcohol and drug use, sexual activity, and fighting.

Chapter One

The challenges facing teenagers have changed significantly in the more than 50 years since these young people gathered for sodas after school. One thing that remains the same, however, is that teenagers must form various types of relationships with many different people—parents and family members, friends, teachers, lovers, and others.

Relationships Revised

The differences between a phrase commonly used by little children and a phrase used by teenagers say a lot about the way relationships change between childhood and adolescence. A child might ask, "Mommy, can you take me on a play date?" while a teenager would say, "Mom, I'm borrowing the car keys, I have a date." The little kid's "mommy" becomes the more grown-up "mom," signaling that the connection between parent and child has matured. The request itself, which changes from "can you take me" to "I'm going," contrasts a young child's utter dependence on parents to the growing self-sufficiency of teenagers. And, of course, there is the obvious difference between the "playdates" of young children and the "dates" that can lead to more adult boyfriend-girlfriend relationships.

The teenage years, that stage between childhood and adulthood, are a time of tremendous change that affects every facet of a young person's life, including his or her relationships with others. Some of those changes come from the inside and can be explained in scientific terms. *Hormones* related to sexuality produce physical changes that include a deepening of the voice for boys, the development of breasts for girls, and the growth of pubic hair for both sexes. Just as significantly, the brain also changes. Scientists have learned that beginning at puberty the human brain's *synapses* and *neurons* rewire themselves, creating new connections between different areas of gray matter, which itself undergoes a growth spurt. "The teenage brain . . . is still very much a work in progress, a giant construction project," writes Barbara Strauch in *The Primal Teen: What the New Discoveries about the Teenage Brain Tell us about Our Kids.* "Millions of connections are being hooked up; millions more swept away. Neurochemicals wash over the teenage brain, giving it a new paint job, a new look, a new chance at life."

That is not all, because there are also changes that come *outside* the person. Teenagers face new pressures and expectations from their parents, their peers, and society in general—so much so that a "teenage culture" has become part of life in Western cultures.

The Rise of Teen Culture

Until the 1950s, the United States had arguably been a land without teenagers. Of course, there have always been young people aged 13 through 19—teenagers in the chronological sense. And everyone has long realized the obvious: that puberty brings physical as well as psychological transformations. Yet those changes alone, which have marked adolescence seemingly forever, did not make teenagers into the distinct social group they form today. In fact, the word "teenager" did not enter the American vocabulary until the 1940s. It was during the post–World War II period that profound changes in U.S. life first gave rise to what has become known as *youth culture*—and with it, the modern teenager.

"Before World War II, Americans went from childhood to adulthood in short order—children were considered fit for work and marriage once puberty was complete," a Gallup report observes. "But with the great surge of prosperity after the war, most middle-class teens did not need to work. They had more leisure time and more money to spend."

When television arrived in U.S. homes during the mid-1950s, it created new images of what it meant to be a modern teenager. Society accepted that fresh new image, and all those young people with spare time and extra money embraced it as their own.

As teenagers grow, existing relationships change. Some may grow apart from their parents while others grow closer.

Not including your parents, is there another adult in whom you can completely trust and confide?

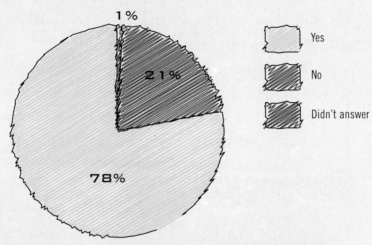

1%

21%

78%

Yes

No

Didn't answer

Is there another person of roughly your own age in whom you can completely trust and confide?

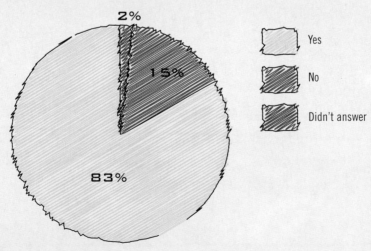

2%

15%

83%

Yes

No

Didn't answer

Poll taken January–March 2004; 785 total respondents age 13–17.
Source: Gallup Youth Survey/The Gallup Organization

"Advertisers coveted them; rock and roll defined them, and sociologists began to study them," explains the Gallup report. "A distinct youth culture was born."

That culture was here to stay, whether based around Elvis Presley in the 1950s, the Beatles in the 1960s, the heavy metal bands of the 1970s, Bruce Springsteen in the 1980s, the "grunge" scene of the 1990s, or the rappers of the new century. And its emphasis on music, fashion, and a rebellious attitude intensified the teen instinct to be different from adults, and in tune with their peers.

New Relationships

All the changes that occur during the teen years—both internal and external—combine to bring a transformation in personality. Teens look at themselves and at their relations with others from a perspective entirely different from that of a pre-adolescent. "Because they are developing the intellectual ability to think abstractly, they can internalize ideas and are becoming aware of an internal personality," says Wendi Ellis-Clark, a counselor in the Boise, Idaho, school system. "Changes that are occurring in their bodies occupy much of their energy. These changes necessitate the formation of new self-images. They spend a large portion of their time in front of mirrors scrutinizing their appearance. They also spend a considerable amount of time with their attention turned inward, scrutinizing the inner self. . . . Because they are in the process of defining themselves, they begin to examine the world in a discriminating fashion. They may seem to be extremely critical of themselves, their parents, peers, siblings, teachers, and others."

It is no surprise that as teens change, so do their relationships with others. Teenagers want more independence from their par-

HOW PARENTS AND FRIENDS INFLUENCE TEENS

Teens were asked: *"For each decision, tell me whether your friends have more influence on you, your parents have more influence, or whether your friends and your parents have about the same amount of influence on you."*

	More influence from		
	Parents	Friends	Same

Parents seem to have more influence...

	Parents	Friends	Same
Whether or not you should go to college	77%	5%	15%
Whether or not to attend religious services	70%	9%	13%
Whether or not you do your homework	66%	15%	11%
What job or career you should be thinking about	63%	5%	24%
Whether or not to drink	50%	24%	20%
Whether or not to have sex with someone	48%	21%	20%

Friends and parents seem to have the same amount of influence...

	Parents	Friends	Same
Whether or not to smoke	47%	26%	18%
Whether or not to date	45%	29%	18%
Whether or not to read	36%	23%	26%

Friends seem to have more influence...

	Parents	Friends	Same
Whether or not to cut classes	33%	50%	10%
With whom to date	25%	44%	21%
The way you wear your hair	19%	47%	21%
What kind of clothes to wear	16%	59%	16%

Poll taken March–June 1997; 491 total respondents age 13–17. Source: The Gallup Organization.

ents than they did before puberty. They become interested in the opposite sex, and preoccupied with their physical appearance. They look for others with whom they can share newfound interests in music, clothing, and just being "hip" in general. They become conscious of themselves as teenagers and may try to behave they way they think teens ought to behave. Parents will impose limits to that much sought-after independence, and teens may rebel. Old childhood friendships end and new peer groups form. And of course, new relationships grow based on sexual attraction, raising all sorts of questions younger kids do not normally confront: does he or she like me? How do I know? What do I do about it?

The relationships teenagers have with their parents and peers — whether as friends or romantic partners — each fulfill a different need. "Adolescents look to peers for association, companionship, and criticism regarding their new social roles," advises Ellis-Clark. "They look to parents for affection, identification, values, and help in solving large problems."

The Gallup Organization is a nationally known firm that has tracked the opinions and attitudes of Americans for decades. Over the past four decades, the Gallup Youth Survey has asked teenagers about their relationships with parents, other adults, peers, and love interests. Although surveys have revealed areas of tension, they have also shown that teenage life in the United States is not as filled with angst and rebellion as many adults might think. Most teenagers tend to be more sexually cautious than the stereotypes seen in movies or music videos, the Gallup Youth Survey has found. Most teens try to find friends who are similar to them while still keeping an open mind about those are different. And most teens love their parents and try to get along with them.

Chapter Two

The teenage years are a time when young people begin to define themselves as individuals. To keep the parent-child relationship from becoming strained, parents must try to understand and respect their childrens' new perspectives while at the same time continuing to provide discipline, structure, and stability in their lives.

Mom and Dad

Twelve-year-old Tracy was a sweet, endearingly awkward California girl who wore pigtails, played with dolls and teddy bears, and was best friends with her mom. Then Tracy became a teenager—and every parent's worst nightmare. She became obsessed with joining the "popular" group at her new junior high school, so she teased her hair, pierced her body, exchanged her plain t-shirts for revealing tube-tops that she stole from stores, and sank into a nightmare of drugs, promiscuity, and self-mutilation. She destroyed her once-loving relationship with her mother and, eventually, destroyed herself.

Lizzie is another young junior high school student, who was as sweet and endearingly awkward as Tracy had once been, and as close to her parents. But the coming of adolescence did not send Lizzie spinning into a teenage hellhole. She stayed out of serious trouble and remained her parents' pride and joy.

Neither Tracy nor Lizzie really exist. Tracy is the bad girl of the film *Thirteen*. Lizzie is the good girl of the "Lizzie McGuire" movie and television series. Yet even though they are fictional characters, they represent two opposite poles of teenagers in their relationships with their parents. In the real world, how many teen-parent relationships are as relaxed and open as Lizzie's relationship with her mom and dad? How many are stormy and headed for disaster, like Tracy's with her mother Mel? Is either of them typical, or are they only extremes?

The relationship between parents and teenagers has long been an American preoccupation. All teens want to show they are grown-up enough to be independent. But the drive for self-sufficiency can explode into conflict with parents. Relationships once based on dependence suddenly become fraught with tension and, in the most extreme cases, open animosity. Parents, on the other hand, see a world of danger and temptation all around their adolescent children. They worry that a loss of communication signals an uncontrolled descent into an abyss from which they may never return.

The Gallup Organization has been conducting surveys on this issue for more than 50 years. In one of the earliest polls, dating from 1954, parents were asked, "There's been a lot of discussion recently about our teenagers getting out of hand. As you see it, what are the main reasons for their acting up?" Respondents blamed parents as well as kids. They said parents were not strict enough in disciplining wayward teens, had too many interests outside the home, and failed to pay enough attention to their children. They said teens had too much freedom, too much money and free time, and were too pampered. Broken homes were also cited as a problem.

Those worries seem familiar to parents today. The question that all teenagers and their parents face is, how are we to build a relationship? Will it be like the doomed Tracy's in *Thirteen*? Like innocent Lizzie McGuire's? Something in between?

Can We Get Along?

Despite the very real tensions that the rise of youth culture has brought between teens and their parents, Gallup polls have consistently found that the vast majority of teenagers say they have a fairly good relationship with mom and dad. Starting in 1977,

A father and son spend quality time together. In general, dads spend much more time with their children today than their own fathers spent with them a generation ago.

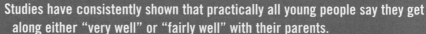

Gallup researchers have been asking teens how they get along with their parents. Every poll has found that between 95 and 98 percent of young people say they get along either "very well" or "fairly well."

More specific survey questions reveal why the parent-child relationship is strong. In 1997 the Gallup Youth Survey found that three of four teens said their parents usually know what is happening at their school. The same percentage also said that teens often talk to adults about things that interest or trouble them. Roughly seven in 10 teens said their family usually eats at least one meal together each day, and 69 percent said they really enjoy mealtime. Sixty-eight percent of teens said an adult is usually home when they get home from school each day. A slight majority of teens (55 percent) said that their families do things together on the weekends. In the 1997 poll, teens also said that they would like to spend more time with their parents. Sixty-eight percent say they want to spend more time with their fathers, and 64 percent want to spend more time with their mothers.

Psychologists say that teens who get along with their parents are happier than teens who do not get along. One study, conducted by the University of Virginia in 1998, found that teens with a strong sense of attachment to their parents are more popular, less likely to be depressed, and less likely to be delinquent. "Adolescents with a secure base with their parents have a 'launching pad' that gives them confidence in themselves and their ability to try new relationships," said Dr. Joseph A. Allen, the professor who led the research. "Teens who don't care about their relationships with parents have lost a 'safety net' that checks their behavior."

Just because Gallup surveys show that most young people get along well with their parents does not mean there aren't strains between parents and their teenage children. In 2000 the Gallup Youth Survey found that 97 percent of teens said they got along with their parents—a figure that is in line with previous surveys. When that number is broken down further, 54 percent said they got along "very well," while 43 percent said they got along "fairly well"—also figures that are similar to the results of previous surveys. But individuals who responded to the surveys also indicated that, while they were not constantly fighting with their parents,

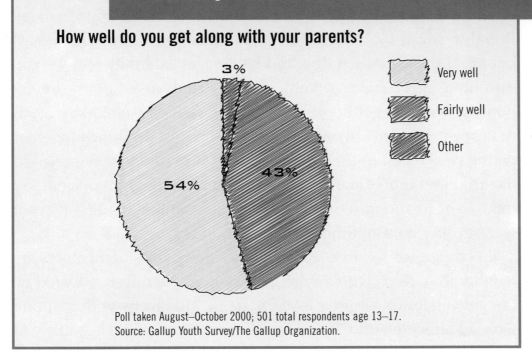

PARENT/TEEN RELATIONSHIPS

How well do you get along with your parents?

3%

54%

43%

Very well

Fairly well

Other

Poll taken August–October 2000; 501 total respondents age 13–17.
Source: Gallup Youth Survey/The Gallup Organization.

neither were their relationships always smooth—which may well be the typical course of events for most teenagers.

"Some so-called negative behavior is considered normal for teenagers as their ideas about the world develop," advises www.teenoutreach.com, a web site put together by young people to help parents understand their teenage children. "Teens tell parents 'I am not you, I am me and here is how I'll show you!' Outlandish hair styles and clothing, messy rooms, listening to loud and 'vulgar' music, or sleeping late are some common ways teens assert their individuality. You can choose to see this kind of behavior as defiance of authority or as a display of integrity. It is important for parents to remember that in rebelling, teens are fulfilling an important psychological need."

Adult experts agree that some differences between teens and their parents are not only inevitable, but may even be a good thing. "Some of the disagreements between parents and teens are necessary and healthy," writes Dr. Michael Tobin, a psychologist who has written several books on family relations. "A teen should push for more freedom and a parent should recognize when his or her teen can handle the responsibility that freedom demands."

Yet in that search for freedom and independence, many young people do not want overly permissive parents. "Please, please, please don't spoil your kids," pleads a 15-year-old on an Internet bulletin board sponsored by the *Minneapolis Star Tribune*. "Even though you may think you're being a good parent for giving them what they want and not punishing them when they misbehave, you will be making life difficult for them later on. . . . You just have to realize that saying no to a child or sending them to their room only helps them in the long run."

Rosalind Wiseman, author of *Queen Bees and Wannabes*, a guide to parenting teenage girls, says this young man is not alone in holding this opinion. "Teens want rules and boundaries," Wiseman writes. "They may rebel, but deep down they know that rules and boundaries make them feel safe, that there's order to the world and that someone's looking out for them."

Still, wanting rules from parents does not mean teens want to be ruled over by parents. That is why in families that get along, teens and their parents work together to come up with mutually acceptable ground rules. "I think very often conflicts develop because parents try to impose things without consulting," says Dr. Peter Marshall, a child psychologist and the author of *Now I Know Why Tigers Eat Their Young: Surviving a New Generation of Teenagers*. "Parents will have the most success in setting limits with their teens if they allow their teens to have some say in the ground rules. It's very important to involve young people in what the rules are and the consequences when they are broken. Sometimes parents worry that teens will come up with a ridiculous consequence like not eating their peas, but really the opposite is true. Teens are usually very responsible when given the chance to take charge over their own lives."

However, even healthy tensions can turn into serious problems unless parents and teens understand each other's perspectives. "Over the last few years, my daughter has become interested in 'Gothic culture,'" wrote one worried father on an Internet bulletin board. "I am becoming somewhat concerned about her behavior as she draws devilish pictures and tells me about how she hates people and the world around her. I realize she is trying to make a statement, but I don't want this getting out of hand." A young person responded, "Wearing black, listening to black/death metal, drawing 'creepy' pictures and not liking some of the rest of the world does not turn people into delinquents. Trust me. Gothic does not automatically make people hate their parents, turn suicidal/homicidal, or drop out of normal life altogether."

In this case, did both the anxious father and the young responder fail to see the other person's perspective? The young person made the point that adopting the external fashions and musical tastes of the Goth culture—or any other subculture that attracts young followers—is not the same as being a delinquent, but did she really address the father's legitimate concerns about a daughter who says she "hates people?" On the other hand, is the father overreacting to what might be nothing more than a temporary adolescent fad? Another parent responded to the question by writing, "My daughter is 13 and enjoys wearing black. She is a really smart and talented kid. Mine also draws creepy pictures. They are actually really good. I will say that I think they grow out of it."

Another bulletin board exchange showed how tensions can ease up as long as parent and teen are willing to work at it. The incident involved an exasperated woman who complained that her 14-year-old daughter stayed in her room sulking and refused to help around the house. The mother explained she finally turned to her older teen, a 17-year-old, for help. "I asked what would be helpful and she replied 'Well duh mom! all you have to do is ask nicely . . . and calmly, and there's a good possibility she'll do something.' Then I asked her why [her younger sister] doesn't emerge out of her room and what she said was a bit shocking. She told me that maybe she is afraid to talk to me because I'm going to get mad."

A teen who embraces the elements of "Goth culture," or a similar lifestyle may be misunderstood by adults who see only the external trappings and overlook the feelings and attitudes of the person underneath the makeup and black clothing.

The mother took the older teen's advice. "About a day later she was out of her room for once and I asked her calmly if she would do the dishes. She just looked at me and said 'okay.' I couldn't believe it!" The mother went on to say, "I also took some time to talk with her in the car when we were on our way to the local store. She said something I didn't agree with about what one of her friends had done, but I just kinda laughed it off with her."

Boomers' Kids

Why was that mother eventually able to "laugh off" things about her daughter, even if it took her a while to start repairing the relationship? Despite a very real difference in age and outlook between parents and teens, many moms and dads today belong to a generation known as the *Baby Boomers*. The Boomers were born between 1946 and 1964, and were teenagers from the late 1950s through the 1970s. During these decades, America's youth culture became so influential that some of its values were embraced by the wider culture of the United States.

That experience makes many contemporary parents familiar with the youth culture that persists today, which, although it has changed in superficial ways, is fundamentally the same. In general, teens and their parents today have more in common than teenage Baby Boomers had in common with their own parents. Today, a mom may still listen to Joni Mitchell albums while her daughter prefers Avril Lavigne CDs, but they both can be said to "rock." And the commonalties go beyond music. Baby Boomers also rebelled as teenagers: Goths and gangstas may be new to them, but they know all about hippies and punk rockers. As a result, William Strauss, who along with Neil Howe co-wrote *Millennials Rising: The Next Great Generation*, told the *New York*

Times in a 2004 article, "We've never seen *tweens* and teens get along with their parents this well." Boomer parents can see the activities of their teenage children not only from an adult perspective, but also as reflections of themselves and their peers when they were young.

Yet that is not always a good thing. At times, teens are ashamed of Boomer parents that act too hip. "I had my nose pierced today," a teen's mother wrote on an internet bulletin board. "When my son got home his comment was complete shock. He told me I was too old to have my nose pierced." The message received one response: "Your son sounds more mature than you. How embarrassing for him. It's highly doubtful that this is just about a nose ring."

Gallup surveys have shown many teens would feel the same way. In fact, some polls indicate that young people today are rebelling against the rebelliousness of their Baby Boomer parents. "Perhaps reacting to what might be described as the excesses of their parents' generation, teens today are decidedly more traditional than their elders were, in both lifestyles and attitudes," writes George H. Gallup Jr. "Gallup Youth Survey data from the past 25 years reveal that teens today are far less likely than their parents were to use alcohol, tobacco, and marijuana. In addition, they are less likely than their parents even today to approve of sex before marriage and having children out of wedlock."

Being with Parents, Talking With Parents

Another way that Baby Boomer culture impacts today's parent-teen relationships is that many Boomer parents, after living through the sexual revolution of the 1960s and 1970s, are willing to speak to their kids about sex. In 2003 the Gallup Youth Survey

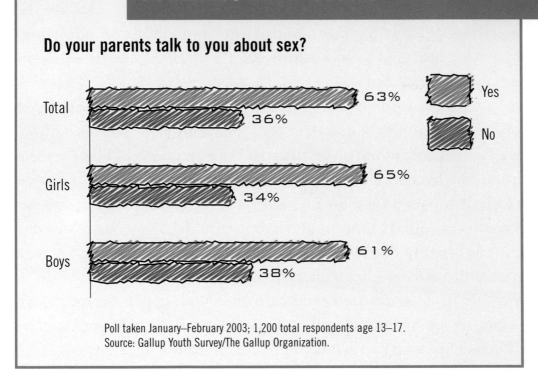

Do your parents talk to you about sex?

Total: Yes 63% / No 36%
Girls: Yes 65% / No 34%
Boys: Yes 61% / No 38%

Poll taken January–February 2003; 1,200 total respondents age 13–17.
Source: Gallup Youth Survey/The Gallup Organization.

asked teens whether their parents are talking to them about sex, or if they are leaving this discussion to their schools. According to these young people, 63 percent of parents do engage in this important discussion. Thirty-six percent said their parents do not speak to them about sex and mostly leave it up to schools.

There were regional differences, the Gallup report noted. "Interestingly, more than two-thirds (67 percent) of teens in the South—an area of the country that is considered to be highly conservative on social issues—report that their parents are talking to them about sex. This is a contrast to the Northeast—an area thought to be more socially progressive—in which only 55 percent of teens report that their parents talk to them about sex." Teens in the West and Midwest reported that 63 percent and 62 percent of parents in each region, respectively, engage teens in discussion about sex.

But gender differences were slight. "Parents appear to be talking about sex to their male and female adolescent children almost equally," notes the Gallup Youth Survey. "Sixty-five percent of teen girls responded that yes, their parents are talking to them about sex and not leaving it to the schools to have this discussion, while 61 percent of teen boys polled gave this response." Nor were older kids more likely than younger ones to have had the discussion: 62 percent of 13- to 15-year-olds said they discussed the issue with their parents, compared to 64 percent of 16- to 17-year-olds.

These numbers suggest that most parents want to talk about sex with their teenage sons and daughters. But do teens want to talk to their parents about this subject? In 1996 the Gallup Youth Survey found that 49 percent of teens were satisfied with the frequency of sexual discussions they had with their parents, while 20 percent said they would like to talk about the issue even more. Only 31 percent wanted to discuss sex "less frequently." The subject teens were least interested in talking about was politics, with 40 percent saying they wanted to hear less about it from their parents. At the other end of the spectrum, the topic teens wanted to discuss more often was family finances—38 percent wanted to know more about money matters.

To be sure, hanging out and talking with parents is not the top choice of teens when they wish to spend a relaxing evening. A 2003 Gallup Youth Survey found the most popular way for teenagers to unwind was to "hang out with friends and family" — yet polls have consistently shown that when friends and family are separated in the question, the preference of teenagers is clearly for their friends. For instance, when teens were asked in 1980 about their favorite ways to spend an evening, "visit with friends" was the top choice with 24 percent, while only 7 percent said "at home with family." In 2001 the gap was even bigger, with 36 percent preferring to spend time with friends compared to 6 percent with family.

Yet Gallup surveys have also shown that teens would like to spend more time with their parents. In 1997, 68 percent said they want to spend more time with their fathers, and 64 percent wanted more time with their mothers. In addition, 71 percent of teens said their family usually eats at least one meal together each day, and 69 percent said they really enjoy mealtime. As one teen put it, "[My favorite way to spend an evening is] at home with my family. I like to cook and I help my parents prepare the meals for all six of us. I play lots of video games with my brothers, but my favorite is when we play board games with all of us, including my parents. We like to watch movies together on TV. We do lots of talking and laughing in the evenings when we are all together."

Family dinners, however, are not what they used to be. "During the early and mid-20th century, when two-parent *nuclear families* were the norm in middle-class America, family dinners at home were a common evening ritual," says another 2003 Gallup Youth Survey. "When dad came home after a hard day's work, mom would have dinner waiting for him. Kids might have after-school activities, but were usually required to be home in time for dinner. In the 21st century, family dinners are more of an evening rarity."

That survey found that 28 percent of adults with children under the age of 18 report that their families eat dinner together at home seven nights a week—down from 37 percent in 1997. And this is less frequently than families surveyed in Great Britain and

Canada, where 38 and 40 percent of families, respectively, eat together every night of the week. In addition, 24 percent of American families say they eat together three or fewer nights a week, compared to 20 percent of Canadian families and 30 percent of British families.

The good news is that three-fourths of U.S. parents say that their families have dinner at home at least four nights a week, as do 80 percent of Canadian parents and 69 percent of British parents. As the Gallup study put it, "In a world as busy as ours, that may be the most today's parents can ask for."

Seeing the Grandparents

How often do those family get-togethers include grandparents or other older relatives? Fairly often, teenagers tell Gallup pollsters. A 2001 survey found that "roughly eight in 10 American teens say they see their own grandparents or the grandparents of close friends at least five or six times per year, while 57 percent said they visited their great aunts, great uncles, older cousins, or other older relatives that frequently."

A considerable number of teenagers also see older people outside the family on a regular basis. Forty-three percent told Gallup they frequently visit friends of their parents or grandparents who are over 70, and 38 percent said they visit elderly neighbors on a regular basis. What is more, a strong majority of teens says they count elderly persons among their close friends. However, this changes with the age of the younger person. Slightly more than three quarters (77 percent) of teens aged 13 to 15 said an older person is a friend, compared to 69 percent of older teens (aged 16 to 17).

These Gallup studies show that that spending time with older people is an important part of many teens' lives. Experts say both

age groups benefit. "The elderly bring wisdom and values into the family equation," says Sue Lawyer-Tarr, a writer who specializes in inter-generational relationships. "They impart a sense of history, continuity of life and the importance of values and community. Great mentors for youth, seniors have knowledge and tolerance for the different stages of children's development." For their part, teenagers, usually full of youthful energy, can make elderly people feel like kids again.

One young person who strongly believes in the importance of relationships between teens and the elderly is Rachel Doyle. When her grandmother died while Rachel was a senior in high school she founded Glamour Gals, a local club in Commack, New York, where young people volunteered to do facials and makeovers for elderly women. Rachel is now 21, and Glamour Gals has expanded to include more than 15 chapters and a website, www.glamourgals.org. "The mature women who participate in the makeover experience acquire a renewed sense of beauty and dignity," says the website. "The participating young adults learn the benefits of community service and leadership while gaining a new respect for the elderly."

Chapter Three

When families fall apart, it is hard on everyone involved. Divorce can be particularly difficult for children, who must try to maintain relationships with their mothers and fathers even after their parents' own relationship is broken.

The Effect of Divorce

Kevin was shocked to hear his mother tell him she and his father were getting divorced. "My heart plunged to the floor," he wrote in an essay about his family crisis. "I thought that my life was going to fall apart. To my surprise, my mother had planned for my sister and me to move, along with her, to Southern California. My dad, however, was going to remain in New Jersey because of his business. My family was splitting apart." The *traumatic* moment when Kevin first heard that his parents were going to live nearly 3,000 miles apart was just the beginning of dramatic changes in his life. Yet through long airplane flights and much soul-searching, the 16-year-old eventually forged a loving relationship with stepparents, stepsiblings, and a new baby half-brother. "I wasn't willing to let [the divorce] ruin my life without putting up a fight, and neither was my family," he says.

Kevin is far from alone in being a teenager forced to cope with the permanent separation of his parents. About half of first marriages in America are expected to end in divorce, according to the U.S. Census Bureau. And even though the rate of divorce has leveled off after reaching a peak in the 1970s and 1980s, the threat of broken families still looms in the future for many teenagers.

In 2001 a Gallup poll found that only a little more than half of teens, 56 percent, lived in a traditional household with both biological parents who were married to each other. Forty-two percent lived with just one parent; in most of those cases, it was because the parents had divorced. Divorce makes millions of teens struggle to build relationships with the parent at home, the parent not at home, and often with new stepparents.

Heading toward Divorce

The problems teens face do not start when they are first told the family will no longer be whole—problems can start before that, when teens overhear their parents arguing. "One day after a long day of running around and playing some games with my friends I walked into our house and my parents were arguing fiercely," a teenager named Robert recalls. "I got scared because I had never heard my parents argue before, and I yelled at them to stop. But they didn't notice that I was there for a long while. Finally they heard me and they stopped yelling at each other. But for the next couple of months they would argue uncontrollably, and I was so scared of what was going to happen I either stayed in my room or I was outside so I wouldn't have to listen to them argue."

Sociologists at Ohio State University have found that teens like Robert begin to have more academic, psychological, and behavioral problems about a year before their parents legally separate.

One teen said the tension and fighting in her home prior to her parents' divorce damaged the relationship she had with her mom and dad. "I lost trust in each one, and developed a 'strong dislike' for both of them, and for their actions," she wrote to the website Teen Advice Online (www.teenadviceonline.org). "I felt like I had to be the adult. I felt that what was happening depressed me, and even left me feeling very alone, as I didn't know how I was supposed to react, or couldn't find anyone at home to understand, or support me through this."

Another young person regretted that because he slacked on his high school academics during the time his parents were fighting, he was rejected by the college he most wanted to attend. "So much stuff was happening I really couldn't see the big picture of things," he confessed on an Internet forum about college life. "I really didn't get how important APs and SATs and such were until around the end of sophomore year, and by that time it was really difficult to advance to higher level courses."

All that parental fighting can be as harmful as the divorce itself. "Divorce is a process, not just a single incident in these children's lives," says Yongmin Sun, the author of the Ohio State study. "It's not accurate to say divorce doesn't matter at all, but it is true that much of the damage to adolescents has already occurred before the divorce."

One way to make that difficult process more bearable, teenagers tell the Gallup Youth Survey, is for parents to keep in mind their childrens' "hierarchy of needs." The 2001 survey found that 78 percent of young people cited a "need to be trusted" and to trust someone in return. "Teens are willing to trust someone, but they don't necessarily know how. After all, trust is a critical element of a successful marriage—but many teens are children of divorce," writes Linda Lyons, Gallup's Education and Youth Editor.

In addition, the 2001 Gallup Youth Survey found that 77 percent of teens had a need to be understood and loved. "Many teens don't feel loved even though their parents say, 'I love you,' or regularly give them hugs," explains Lyons. "They need to 'feel' love to feel loved—they need to feel nurtured as well as cared for." This is true even when mom and dad are arguing their way to a divorce.

Coping with Divorce

The physical separation of divorce, of course, ends the day-to-day fighting between parents at home and eases some of the tension that teens feel when they see their moms and dads argue. Yet it is just as obvious that the actual breakup of a family brings its own forms of heartache. Bitter *custody* fights can have a devastating effect on teenagers. Most painful is when parents expect their children to take sides.

"My mom made me feel like a traitor since I had chosen Daddy over Mommy," one teenager wrote on the internet youth magazine www.youthcomm.com. "She made me feel I was the one tearing the family apart. It made me angry that she would even think that I was choosing one parent over the other. It's not that I loved my father more than I did her. It was just such a relief not having to take care of my sisters or clean up the house anymore. I was just doing what I felt was best for myself. If I had one wish it would be that my mom and dad loved one another again. I would like my family back together. The reality is that will never happen, and that has to be the harshest realization of all."

Having parents who live in different places is also difficult. Sixteen-year-old Matt Crellin told the *Maine Sunday Telegram* about his trouble relating to his divorced parents, who live in different towns. "It's very rare that I wake up in the same bed two nights in a row," he said. "I never really get to unpack. It almost feels like you're traveling between two hotel rooms." To make matters worse, he said, his parents continued to fight after the divorce. "My brother and I would be constantly stuck in the middle. My parents couldn't even carry on a conversation, so we'd be the messengers. 'Mom says this.' 'Dad says that.' I felt pushed directly into the whole maelstrom of the divorce."

Although Matt Crellin's parents lived in different towns, their homes were relatively close. For other teens, visiting mom or dad involves a long trip. After Nick Sheff's parents divorced, his mother moved to Los Angeles. He lived with her during summers and

Feelings of guilt, abandonment, and resentment are common among young people whose parents divorce.

spent long weekends at her house, while the rest of the time he lived with his father in San Francisco. "I began flying between two cities and two different lives. . . . Some people love to fly, but I dreaded the trips," he wrote in an essay that appeared in *Newsweek* magazine.

And it wasn't just air travel that made Nick's joint-custody arrangement so difficult for him. He found himself having to build entirely new relationships—not just with his parents, but with nearly everyone important in his life. "Arriving in L.A., I was excited to see my mom and stepdad," he wrote. "It had been almost three months since my last visit. But it took a while to adjust. Each set of parents had different rules, values and concerns. . . . When I'm in northern California, I miss my mom and stepdad. But when I'm in L.A., I miss hanging out with my friends, my other set of parents and little brother and sister."

As many as 25 percent of teens whose parents divorce end up depressed or abuse dangerous substances, according to the National Institute of Mental Health. Relationship professionals advise parents that they can help their children avoid these problems if they can keep the divorce from becoming too bitter. "Whatever the level of conflict or hostility you feel toward your ex-spouse," Wake Forest University professor of psychology Christy Buchanan advises divorced parents, "try to isolate it so the children are not drawn into it." Parents throughout the nation have taken that advice by taking part in seminars where they learn to protect their kids from the anger they may feel toward one another. At one such session in Atlanta, a social worker showed divorcing parents the artwork of kids whose parents were splitting. "Divorce is like getting stabbed by 1,000 knives," one child had written above a red stick figure. Some parents wept.

These seminars seem to be doing some good. A study sponsored by the National Institute of Mental Health found that teens whose parents attended "divorce sessions" were half as likely to develop mental disorders as teenagers whose parents did not get professional help.

Professional help is also available for teens whose parents are getting divorced. "A teen needs a great deal of support even though they may protest that they are self-sufficient and independent," says California psychologist Debra Moore. Counselors often assure guilt-ridden teens that they are not at fault for their parents' decision to divorce, and help young people find a way to accept the inevitable separation. "As soon as possible, the teen needs to get on with their own lives, to resume their normal adolescent activities, and to get back to being preoccupied with typical teenager concerns," Dr. Moore says.

Is Marriage in Teens' Future?

"A teen's fundamental attitudes about marriage and about themselves can be forever changed by divorce and the events that happen in the years afterwards," says Dr. Moore. "[They] may be terrified that they will repeat their parents' marital failure. They wonder if they are capable of sustaining a marriage themselves."

One result of such apprehensions is that teenagers tell the Gallup Youth Survey it is too easy to get a divorce. Fifty-five percent of teens surveyed agreed with that statement in 1977, when the divorce rate was higher than it is today. But by 2001 the number of teenagers who said getting a divorce was too easy had risen to 77 percent. "Morality issues aside, it is not hard to speculate as to why teens are so likely to believe that divorce comes too easily in American society," a Gallup report noted. "A huge percentage of today's teens are growing up with divorced parents. Many teens with divorced parents probably dream of having a 'traditional' family in which their parents are still together, and teens with married parents are unlikely to enjoy the thought of their parents divorcing." More teens are also telling Gallup that parents who divorce tried first to save their marriages. Only 29 percent of young people thought this was the case in 1977, compared to 40 percent in 2001. Those percentages show, however, that more than half of teens believe parents need to work harder at saving troubled marriages.

Despite the issue of divorce and the heartbreak it causes many young people, Gallup Youth Surveys throughout the years have found that nothing has diminished teenagers' desire to ultimately get married and have children. In fact, the surveys show a steady increase in both aspirations since the divorce rate peaked in the late 1970s. In 1977, 84 percent of teens surveyed said they wanted to get married some day, and 79 percent said they wanted children. In 1989, 90 percent indicated they saw marriage in their future, and 84 percent expected to have children. By 2001, the percentages had increased even more — in that survey, 93 percent wanted to marry and 91 percent wanted to have children. The results remained the same even when broken down by gender or on ethnic lines.

An analysis of the data by the Gallup Organization attributed the steadily growing enthusiasm, in part, to education. "Florida is the first state in the nation to require a course in relationships and marriage for all high school graduates," the report said. "Elsewhere in the nation, teachers and others who work with school-age children are incorporating units on healthy relationships into existing curricula or offering marriage and relationship courses as electives."

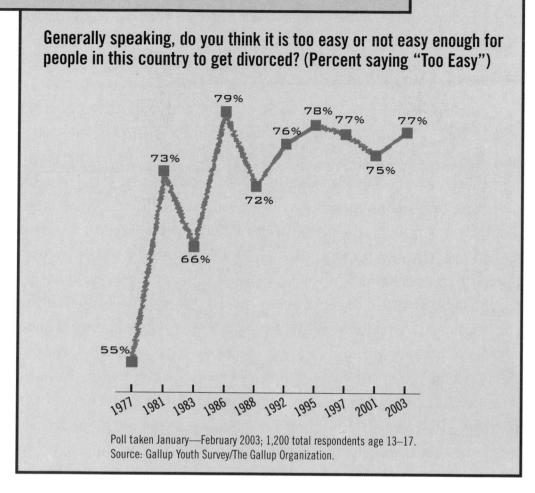

Generally speaking, do you think it is too easy or not easy enough for people in this country to get divorced? (Percent saying "Too Easy")

Poll taken January—February 2003; 1,200 total respondents age 13–17.
Source: Gallup Youth Survey/The Gallup Organization.

A second factor, Gallup said, "may be the expectation among young people that they will marry somewhat later in life than their forebears. According to the U.S. Census, the average age of marriage now is 27 for men and 25 for women—an increase of nearly five years since the 1960s. With less social pressure to marry at an early age, teens may feel they have more freedom to wait until they're emotionally and economically prepared for marriage." The report concludes, "Whether it's coursework, the determination to reverse a trend that created turmoil in many of their parents' lives, or just the universal optimism of youth, American teens remain largely united in their resolve to build successful marriages and family life."

When Parents Never Marry

Although most young people are interested in getting married and having children, sometimes the children come without the marriage. In 2002, 34 percent of children were born to women who had never married, according to the National Center for Health Statistics. Sixty-three percent of those moms had never graduated from high school and only 4 percent had college degrees. These factors contribute to a high poverty rate for families with children born out of wedlock.

Teenagers whose parents never married face problems that the children of divorced parents never face. Teens whose parents have divorced often maintain a relationship with both parents, but many teens born out of wedlock never even meet their fathers. And studies have shown that growing up without ever having a father figure can be damaging. For instance, boys living in father-less homes are two to three times more likely to be involved in crime and drop out of school. The problem is particularly critical in the black community. According to the National Center for Health Statistics, among black women who gave birth during 2002, 68 percent were unmarried. By comparison, the NCHS reported lower figures among Hispanic women (43 percent were unmarried) and non-Hispanic white women (23 percent).

The Gallup Youth Survey has found that teenagers themselves are unsure about how having a relationship with a father can affect their future. In a 2000 survey, 49 percent of teens agreed that boys who grow up with a father are more likely to be successful as adults, and almost 45 percent said they are more likely to be happy. But roughly one quarter disagreed on both questions, and another quarter said they did not know. In addition, 42 percent agreed that boys who grow up with their father at home are less likely to get into trouble with the law, but 41 percent disagreed. Teens are also unsure about a father's influence with regard to dissuading substance abuse. Thirty-two percent agreed that boys growing up with a father at home are less likely to have a problem

Teen pregnancy is a major problem in the United States. Studies show that approximately 900,000 unmarried teenage girls give birth each year. Unfortunately, many of these children must grow up without their biological father being involved in their lives.

with drug or alcohol use but almost half (46 percent) disagreed with this statement.

Another problem is that over the past 30 years the number of teens who become unmarried parents has skyrocketed. In 1970 about 22 out of every 1,000 unmarried girls between the ages of 15 and 19 gave birth; by 2004 that figure was up to more than 35 out of every 1,000. Many studies have shown that children of unwed teenagers are even more likely than children of unwed adults to live in poverty, drop out of school, or go to jail. One positive trend, however, is that the number of births by unmarried teenagers has begun to decline over the last few years. While the rate in 2004 was much higher than it was in the 1970s, the rate has gone down every year since 1994, when it hit a peak of about 46 per thousand.

Relationships Between Parents and Children

Teens who live in divorced families often have one relationship with their mothers, and a different relationship with their fathers. This is also true of teens who still live with both of their parents. Gallup surveys taken over the last 30 years consistently show that well over 75 percent of teens say they get along better with one parent than with the other. Most of the time, teens get along better with their mothers. In a 2000 Gallup Youth Survey, for instance, 56 percent of teens said they got along better with their moms, while 25 percent said they got along better with their fathers. Just 16 percent said they got along equally well with both parents.

In some cases, the difference simply comes down to the personality of the individuals involved. "I get along better with my dad because he's just a lot more easy going than my mom," wrote one 17-year-old on her online diary. "Plus we have the same slightly demented sense of humor and my mom finds neither of us funny!" Still, in many families gender plays a direct role in the closeness of the relationship. One investigation by Great Britain's Cambridge University found mothers and their teenage daughters on average had one 15-minute-long argument every two-and-a-half days, while boys and their moms argued, on average, for six minutes every four days. Fathers and daughters did not argue too much, said the study, but that was because when there is tension, daughters tend to give dads "the cold shoulder and ignore them."

The study also said that arguing may actually be good for relationships, particularly between moms and daughters, because teenage girls often use arguments as a way of communicating. "The [fights] often start from absolutely nothing. But they rapidly escalate to where the daughter is saying 'I hate you' and the mother is upset," said Dr. Terri Apter, author of the Cambridge study. "But . . . daughters often use arguments to update mothers about their lives and what they are doing and what is important to them. Arguments . . . sometimes keep the relationship going."

Most experts agree that parents of different genders tend to have different parenting styles. "Fathers tend to observe and enforce rules systematically and sternly, which teach children the objectivity and consequences of right and wrong," says Glenn T. Stanton, the author of several books on family issues. "Mothers tend toward grace and sympathy in the midst of disobedience, which provide a sense of hopefulness." Moms and dads also communicate with their teens in different ways. "Fathers' talk tends to be more brief, directive, and to the point," Stanton says. "[Fathers] also make greater use of subtle body language and facial expressions. Mothers tend to be more descriptive, personal, and verbally encouraging. Children who do not have daily exposure to both

Although arguments generally are not pleasant, they may help relationships between teen girls and their mothers. A Cambridge University study found that teens will use an argument over a superficial issue as a way to communicate deeper feelings or concerns.

will not learn how to understand and use both styles of conversation as they grow."

The gender of the parent is not the only factor—the gender of child also affects how relationships are formed, because psychologists believe that parents treat their teen kids differently depending on whether they are boys or girls. For instance, parents may set up different expectations. One study found that "daughters more than sons are encouraged to attend to others' needs, to conform to others' expectations." Or parents may monitor the behavior of their daughters strictly, while allowing their sons to "get away" with more, the study found.

Teenagers themselves may relate differently to their parents depending on gender, with boys often getting along better with their dads and girls with their moms. For instance, upon hitting adolescence girls often begin to feel distant from fathers and believe dad does not meet their emotional needs. "There are lots of things that can begin to interfere with a dad's closeness to his daughter," says social worker Jean Walbridge, advice columnist at www.parentingadolescents.com. "The daughter begins to want a little independence—she is growing up and gradually may demand more freedoms, she's not 'his little girl' any longer, and some dads have a hard time making that adjustment. The daughter is developing into a young woman physically, and many dads just find it hard to make the transition from seeing their daughter as 'a child.'" On the other hand, says noted gender issues researcher Shere Hite, "a number of girls feel they have a special secret closeness with their fathers, a special relationship, that they are really their father's 'favourite.'"

For their part, boys influenced by the teen culture of "macho cool" may not believe their mothers can teach them how to be a "real man." Yet child psychologist Dr. William Pollack believes that women are well able to teach their teenage sons how to become men. "Since young boys are taught that staying close to their mothers is something 'shameful,' one of their natural responses is to turn to their fathers for love," he wrote in *Real Boys:*

Which of your relatives do you feel best understands you?

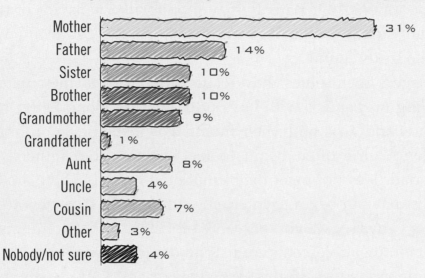

Relative	
Mother	31%
Father	14%
Sister	10%
Brother	10%
Grandmother	9%
Grandfather	1%
Aunt	8%
Uncle	4%
Cousin	7%
Other	3%
Nobody/not sure	4%

Which relative do you consider to be the best role model?

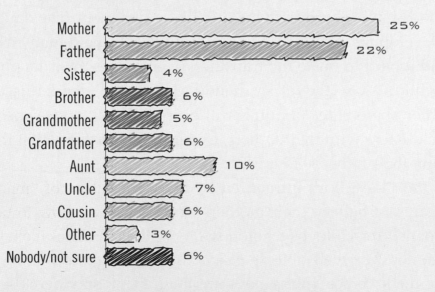

Relative	
Mother	25%
Father	22%
Sister	4%
Brother	6%
Grandmother	5%
Grandfather	6%
Aunt	10%
Uncle	7%
Cousin	6%
Other	3%
Nobody/not sure	6%

Poll taken March–June 1996; 502 total respondents age 13–17.
Source: Gallup Youth Survey/The Gallup Organization.

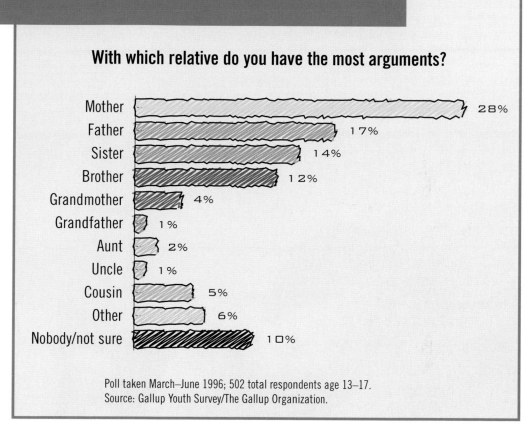

With which relative do you have the most arguments?

Relative	Percent
Mother	28%
Father	17%
Sister	14%
Brother	12%
Grandmother	4%
Grandfather	1%
Aunt	2%
Uncle	1%
Cousin	5%
Other	6%
Nobody/not sure	10%

Poll taken March–June 1996; 502 total respondents age 13–17.
Source: Gallup Youth Survey/The Gallup Organization.

Rescuing Our Sons from the Myths of Boyhood. "Yet for some boys, mothers may offer a special kind of nurturing, loving interaction that even the most caring father may not be able to replicate."

Yet Gallup polls have shown that at least when it comes to their fathers, teens know what they want — and that most teens get it. In a 1998 survey, 91 percent of teens said it was important for dad to "show respect and caring for his children's mother," with 75 percent agreeing that their "own father definitely does this." Eighty five percent said it was important at least once a week to hear their fathers say he loved them, and 66 percent reported that their father did exactly that.

Chapter Four

With adolescence comes an attraction to members of the opposite sex. The blossoming of young romance is very exciting, but feelings of uncertainty and awkwardness can also make this time stressful for many young people.

The Opposite Sex

It is not just the birds and the bees. It is also lizards and lobsters, goldfish and goats—even plants and algae. The urge to reproduce is not only as old as life itself, but it is also essential to life. It begins with finding a mate. And even though neither plants nor algae actually have a drive to attract a partner, just about all higher life forms do in one way or another. Many birds and mammals display those urges through *courtship rituals*. For instance, a male red-tailed hawk looking to impress a female will fly lazy circles high in the sky, and then dive down at lightning speed; if she accepts him, she joins him in mid-air and the pair swoops down together with locked talons. Then they go off together to build a nest.

For animals like the red-tailed hawk, mating behaviors are *instinctive*. Animals do not need to think about how to attract members of the opposite sex—they just do it. The actions they take are programmed into their *genetic code*. But although

During adolescence, young people begin to form their first romantic relationships.

sexual desire is written into the genetic code of humans—just as it is in the genetic code of animals—there are no instructions on how to go about finding and then attracting a member of the opposite sex. People must take conscious and deliberate actions to do that. They must think about what they want to accomplish, make a plan, then act on it.

Figuring out what to do can be a problem. While hawks will always know to swoop and twist to find a mate, humans do not always know how to start a romantic relationship. "I never had a girl friend and I am 16. I am just very shy," wrote one young man on a website devoted to teen dating issues. "I never had any guts to come up to a girl and even talk to her about anything! If a girl comes up to me and asks me a question I usually give a stupid reply and mumble something." Even though this young man did not know how to make himself attractive to the opposite sex, asking questions was his very human way to come up with a plan to find a girlfriend.

Wanting to be attractive begins in adolescence, with the first stirrings of sexual desire. Of course, how teens go about finding a mate varies from society to society. In the United States, it starts with dating. When the Gallup Youth Survey asked teens about their romantic lives in 1977, more than half of the teenagers surveyed (61 percent) said they had their first date before they reached the age of 16, and about one-third (35 percent) confessed they had kissed on their first date. Today the numbers may be different, yet teenagers still shop for clothing, style their hair, and sharpen their social skills to impress the opposite sex. And even though many teens may not realize it, they also follow a social code that determines what is "cool" and what is "uncool" in boy-girl relationships.

Romance, American Teen Style

Animals' mating rituals do not change—hawks have been locking talons the same way for eons. In contrast, American teenagers have *dating* rituals, with "rules" that evolve through the years as society changes. But that very flexibility can bring confusion to teenagers trying to figure out what is socially acceptable, and what is not, when they try to form romantic relationships. For instance, what do teenagers mean when they say they are "going steady" with someone? In a 1977 Gallup poll, 32 percent of girls and 23 percent of boys said they were presently "going steady." The term still exists. But some teens say the relationship it describes is different from what it meant a generation ago.

"When someone says, 'go out,' I think 'boyfriend and girl-friend.' My parents think it means just hanging out at the movies, mall, or someplace," a 16-year-old girl commented on www.teenadviceonline.org. One teen answered, "I also think of the phrase 'going out' to mean the whole exclusive relationship thing, same as you. To [parents], what we think of as 'going out' with someone was 'going steady." Another teen, a 16-year-old boy, agreed with the "new" definition, adding that today there is too much pressure to turn casual dating into steady relationships. "At school, as soon as you go on one date somehow it is assumed that you are going out," he wrote. "There are a couple of girls that I would like to date, but I don't necessarily want a relationship." At least one girl agreed with him. "The 'art' of dating seems to have disappeared. . . . you can just ask a girl if she wants to go to a movie with you or just hang out. That doesn't necessarily mean 'do you want to be my girlfriend with our names engraved in stone.'"

Another question that leaves some teens perplexed is, who takes the initiative? One shy high school senior asked www.teen-wire.com, "I really want a boyfriend but I am to scared to just go up to a boy and talk to him if I like him. How I can get over that fear and get a boy that I like to ask me out?" Answered the editors, "A lot of girls feel like they are supposed to wait for a guy to ask them out or make the first move. But this isn't true. It is totally fine for a girl to ask out a guy." Americans increasingly agree, according to Gallup polls. In 1950, Gallup found that only 29 percent of Americans thought it was acceptable for a girl to phone a boy and ask him out for a date, while 62 percent considered it unacceptable. Fifty years later opinions had completely changed: 70 percent said it was fine for a girl to call a boy, while 28 percent still followed the traditional view. Interestingly, 80 percent of men said it was okay for a girl to ask a boy out, compared to 62 percent of women.

Once the date is on, regardless of who invited who, there is another question: who pays? "Two generations ago, the man was expected to. A generation later, women paid their own way. Today, many young ladies silently embrace the notion that the guy should pay if he can afford it—but guys don't seem to have

Many teens are nervous about dating, but it doesn't need to cause anxiety.
Experts say the best advice is to do something you enjoy, and be yourself.

caught on," reported an article on dating that appeared in the *Washington Post*. It told the story of a college student who finally agreed to go on a dinner date with a guy who had been pursuing her since high school. He told her he would pay. But when the bill came out, the girl recalled, "It lay on the table for 10, 15, then 20 minutes. I went to the bathroom and when I came back, it was still there . . . If he had told me from the beginning he couldn't pay it all, that would have been fine. But as it was, he blew it."

Unrequited Love

Songs like Avril Lavigne's "Sk8er Boi," about a snobby girl who rejected a boy she liked because of the way he dressed, are nothing new. The theme of romantic rejection has been a staple of pop music ever since singers started to make records. And that is because unrequited love has caused teenage heartbreak seemingly forever.

In a Gallup Youth Survey taken in 2001, more than three quarters of teens said they had a "very strong" need to be loved and to be trusted. An earlier survey, taken in 1977, found that 61 percent of girls said they were "in love," compared to just 42 percent of boys. Yet nobody needs poll numbers to know that some people who want to be loved are in love with someone who does not love them back.

"I didn't even realize myself that I was falling for this guy until one day I was visiting at his house and he asked me to brush off some stuff that had fallen on his shirt. Just actually helping him clean off the sleeve and standing close to him sent such a jolt through me," says one girl named Jenny. "Then he showed me photos of him and his girlfriend and told me, pointedly, that he had a friend he thought I would like. I got the message. That was so awful; but obviously just because I had to respect his feelings on the matter didn't mean mine were getting any easier. I wrote a 6-

page essay on how I felt and then tore it out of my journal. There hasn't been a day since then that I have not thought of him."

Falling in love with someone who does not return the feelings can happen for any number of reasons. It can be that one person is already in a relationship, as in Jenny's situation. It can be because of a difference in social class, real or perceived, like between Avril Lavigne's baggy-clothed skateboarder and the ballet-dancing girl whose snooty friends all "stuck up their nose" at him. Or it can simply be that there is no attraction. Whatever the case, it can be sheer agony for teenagers. They may daydream

When feelings of attraction are unreturned, teens may start to wonder if there is something wrong with them. These moments of self-doubt are shared by many young people.

about holding hands with the beloved or listen to sad music. Sometimes it can even result in depression.

Unfortunately, the problem is not easy to fix. "You can not make somebody love you. You can't even make them like you. There are no magic spells or secret tricks that will make a person suddenly feel for you the way you feel for them. Love doesn't work like that," says Mike Hardcastle, host of a teenage advice web page. Hardcastle goes on to advise heartbroken teens to think about the future, difficult though it may be. "Love, when it is real and returned, is one of the most amazing feelings you will ever experience," he says. "Although it is hard to accept that this person doesn't return your feelings, it may help you to know that the pain you now feel will be erased from your heart when you find someone who does love you back."

Author Kimberly Kirberger says in *Teen Love: On Relationships* that the first step in overcoming the suffering about unrequited love should be to learn to love oneself. "We think that everyone else is happy with the way he or she is. . . . Here is a little secret. Everybody is insecure. Everybody judges himself or herself harshly, and everybody struggles with the concept of loving himself or herself. The good news is that once we become aware of the way we treat ourselves, we can change it. The most worthwhile goal you can set for yourself is one of self-love and self-acceptance."

Breaking up Is Hard to Do

Another theme as popular in music as "unrequited love"—and one that causes as much real life teenage anguish—is "breaking up." While in one case the relationship never started, in the other romance does blossom, only to be ended by one partner to the distress of the other. It is all part of the process most teenagers will experience as they mature, because when teens begin to date they are taking only the first step in the search for a lifelong partnership. Even though teens sometimes think that a particular boyfriend of girlfriend is "it," they may later want to break up, or find themselves being told by the other person that the relationship is over. The partner who decides to break up will be disappointed that things did not work out, and the partner who wanted to remain in the relationship will feel as if his or her heart is forever broken.

Why do relationships end? One reason is cheating. Few dating couples will stay together if one person decides to go out with

Today, the Internet has become a place where teens can find answers to their questions or problems about love and romance. Although researching a problem anonymously on the computer can be less awkward for teens, it may also reduce the traditional advisory role of parents or other adults.

someone else. There are other causes, too. A survey of 150 couples on an Internet dating site found three reasons most often cited. One reason was feeling trapped. "Most people want intimacy and connection in a dating relationship, but not at the price of reasonable freedom," said the study. A second reason the survey found that relationships end was that the people did not have enough in common. As many relationships progress, the study said, one or both partners "discovered that . . . their attitudes, beliefs, values, or interests simply did not jive, whether it involved deeply held religious convictions or something as seemingly frivolous as an unmatched sense of humor." The third reason was lack of supportiveness. The people surveyed "complained their dates were not encouraging, sympathetic, or understanding."

Sometimes, too, one partner simply stops liking the other. "I just broke up with my boyfriend," an eighth grader wrote to teen advice syndicated columnist Lucie Walters. "He had asked me if I really liked him, and I responded that I didn't know. I ended up breaking up with him. I felt guilty going out with him for no reason. I guess he's kind of mad at me because he has liked me since the fourth grade."

As this young girl's feelings of guilt show, initiating the breakup is difficult. And when the other person does not want to let go, it can be harder. "I met this guy at school that seemed really nice and I thought it would be good to get to know him better," one teen asked www.askhearbteat.com. "After spending some time around him I realized that I was not really that interested. He is nice and all, but he's not for me. I politely told him that I was not interested in him and now I can't seem to get rid of him!" The website's teen romance advisors replied she needed to get tough: "Start by asking him if he understands what 'not interested' means. Correct his interpretation since he doesn't seem to be clear. Then ask him what he thinks he is going to accomplish by calling you all the time when you aren't interested in dating him. Tell him he needs to be calling someone that may be interested in seeing him romantically because you aren't."

Of course, that kind of tough talk is bound to be, well, tough on her former boyfriend. And so it goes—as hard as it is to be the one who breaks up with someone, it is harder still to be on the receiving end. Yet young people with broken hearts can take comfort, because there is truth in the cliché "time heals all wounds." Many experts give practical advice on how to get over the end of a romantic relationship. Teenwire.com advises, "Do something physical like going on a long bike ride or a fast run. Many people find that being out in nature helps them get a handle on their emotions. When you start to feel better, reach out to people and find things to do. Join some new group, call three people every day, make plans for the weekend, take up running, read a book. Your days will go by much faster if you fill them with things you like to do. You'll meet new people and you'll spend less time thinking about your old relationship."

Experts also say that even teens who are going steady should keep in mind that they are still young, because being in love at 16 does not guarantee the couple will be together happily ever after. "Sure, it CAN happen, just like lightning can strike the same place twice," say the relationship experts at www.askheartbeat.com in response to a 16-year-old who asked what the chances were that she and her boyfriend of two years would spend the rest of their lives together. "But the chances . . . aren't on your side. People change too much in their teens and 20s, and most of the time what we think we want at 18 is something completely different at 30! . . . You may have dated a few people, but honey you haven't had the experiences of a grown woman and therefore your knowledge of men, relationships, the variety of human interactions and growth you could experience is extremely limited. He is a big fish to you because you are both swimming in a small pond."

Young Sexual Conservatives

Teenagers may begin dating in small ponds, but sooner or later they will discover there are plenty of fish in the sea—then head out to where the ocean is wide open and deep. The problems come when they do not know how to swim, and the water goes over their heads. Why are they in danger of drowning? Because the sexual revolution that began in the late 1960s changed the values of the entire nation and put teenagers in the position of having to make decisions about having sex—the kind of decision that two generations ago had an almost universally accepted answer: no.

In 1969 a Gallup poll showed that premarital sex between consenting adults was still taboo in those years: two-thirds of adult Americans said it was morally wrong. But by 1985, 52 percent said premarital sex was acceptable, and by 2003 that figure had risen to 60 percent. Such profound changes could not help but also influence what today's teens think about sex. For instance, a 2001 Gallup Youth Survey poll found that 57 percent of teens said "sex between an unmarried man and woman" was "morally acceptable." Three years later, 69 percent of teens age 13 to 17 told the Gallup Youth Survey they approved of couples living together before marriage. "These numbers are not surprising, given the prevalence of unmarried couples living together in America today," Gallup reported at the time. "According to the last U.S. census, 3.8 million unmarried couples were reportedly *cohabitating*.

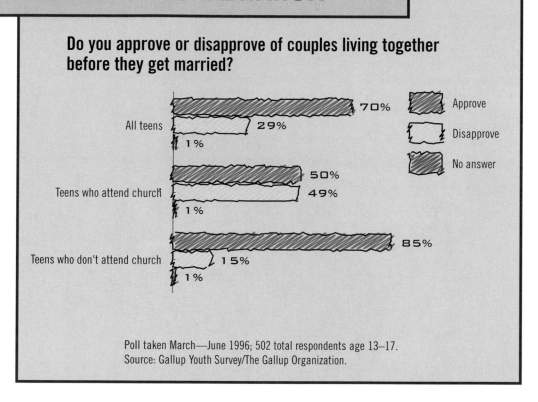

Do you approve or disapprove of couples living together before they get married?

All teens
70% Approve
29% Disapprove
1%

Teens who attend church
50%
49%
1%

Teens who don't attend church
85%
15%
1%

Approve
Disapprove
No answer

Poll taken March—June 1996; 502 total respondents age 13–17.
Source: Gallup Youth Survey/The Gallup Organization.

Given this reality, it is not surprising that a majority of teens approve of couples living together prior to marriage, and it is not improbable that they themselves may become part of this growing trend in the future."

Those polls reflect young people's views about the sexual lives of adults—the first survey specifically referred to men and women, not teens, while the second specifically mentioned "cohabitation," a household arrangement that teens living at home with their parents are unlikely to take up. But other Gallup surveys shed light on what teens think of premarital sex between teens themselves. And, perhaps surprisingly, it turns out that sizeable numbers believe it is not a good idea for teens to have sex, even if they say it is okay for adults. A Gallup Youth Survey taken in 2001 showed that fully 59 percent of teenagers would "feel guilty" about having premarital

Young people in a romantic relationship often feel pressure to "go all the way."

sex. Girls were more likely than boys to say they would feel guilty, by a margin of 66 percent for girls versus 53 percent for boys.

On the other hand, guilty feelings about having sex ranked at the bottom of the list of nine moral issues measured in the poll, (the top two guilt-inducers were "neglecting parents when they are old" with 92 percent, and "stealing something" with 88 percent), which according to a Gallup analysis, suggests "that most teens do not view [premarital sex] as morally egregious as neglecting their parents or stealing," This brings up the question of how many teens lead sexually active lives, even if it makes them feel guilty.

Some teens feel pressure to make that decision at an early age. "I am 13 years old and in love with my boyfriend! But the other day he asked me if I wanted to have sex. I do but I don't. See, I love him SOOOOO much but I don't want to lose my virginity! PLEASE HELP," a girl asked www.teenwire.com.

"Jumping into the sack before you're ready can cause you grief. You can love someone, but not be ready to have sex," she was advised. "One of the most important things you can do is let your boyfriend know how you feel. Be clear with him and explain how you feel about sex and why you're not ready. Be honest and firm. You can say 'I've made up my mind to wait' or 'I really love you, but I'm not ready to have sex'" The site's advisors also noted, "It may seem as though everyone your age is having sex. This can make you feel that you should be, too. But the truth is that only about half of high school students have ever had intercourse. Far fewer have it on a regular basis. Many kids who have had sex wish that they had waited."

A study by the Center for Disease Control suggests more teens are making the decision to wait. In 1991 54 percent of high school students admitted to having had sex, but by 2003 that figure had gone down to 47 percent. In addition, the number of teens who said they had four or more sexual partners decreased from 19 percent to 14 percent. An earlier CDC study, done in 2001, found that the decline in sexual activity over the previous decade held true for young people of different ethnic backgrounds. The largest reduction was among black teens: 81 percent said they were sexually active in 1991 compared to 61 percent ten years later. The reported sexual activity of white teens decreased over the same period from 50 percent to 43 percent, and for Hispanic teens the figure dropped from 53 percent to 48 percent.

These figures match what several Gallup Youth Surveys have found teens say about sex. In the 2001 Gallup Youth Survey in which 59 percent of teens approved of premarital sex between consenting adults, 42 percent said they disapproved—a figure higher than the 38 percent of adults who said they disapproved. This suggests that teens may be more conservative than their elders when it comes to sexual matters. What is more, the percentage was higher than it was in 1977, when only 30 percent of teens thought premarital sex between unmarried men and women was wrong— suggesting that, at least among teens, the trend is the opposite of what one might expect given the sexual revolution.

Why has this trend changed? Experts cite fear of AIDS and other sexually transmitted diseases, for one thing. "When asked in 1988 what they felt was the most urgent health problem facing this country, 57 percent of all teens named HIV/AIDS," reads a report by the Gallup Poll. "Although that level of concern had declined to 14 percent in [a 2001] poll, teens are more likely today than they were prior to the advent of Acquired Immune Deficiency Syndrome (AIDS) to be educated about the dangers of sexually transmitted diseases." There is also more sex education in schools. "Eighty-nine percent of students in America's public schools take a sex education course between 7th and 12th grade . . . one-third of schools in the United States teach abstinence-only sex education" said a 2002 Gallup Youth Survey report. Or it could be a form of rebellion—if some adults think sex outside of marriage is fine, some teens might take the opposite view.

Chapter Five

Social groups (or cliques) can be both good and bad. They give the teens who belong to such a group a sense of security, community, and confidence. However, teens who are excluded may feel depressed, resentful, and lonely.

Friends, Cliques, and Peer Pressure

When Jake Thorud moved to a new high school in Illinois his sophomore year, he did not know anyone. But not seeing familiar faces made it easier to see something else: the different *cliques* within the school. "I first noticed the Punks because of the trademark clothes they wear," he wrote in an essay for on www.tolerance.org. "Dressed mainly in black with shirts advertising each of their favorite punk bands, the Punks talk to other Punks. Next, I noticed the Jocks. Nearly all of the Jocks participate in football and stick out from the crowd by wearing their uniforms on the day of the big game. After that I noticed the Preps—since Preps are not always wearing the same thing, they are more difficult to pick out. Although they are usually dressed nice in their polo shirts and khakis, preps wear a variety of different clothing. Preps are often distinguished by their snobby attitudes or high economic status. Finally, I started to make out another group. On the opposite side of the spectrum from the Preps, I found the Nerds. Frequently noted by their high intelligence, Nerds usually will not usually wear the newest or trendy clothes." Almost no one in those groups talked to people in other groups. And if Jake made friends with people in one group, people in a different group stopped speaking to him.

Punks, jocks, preps, and nerds. Headbangers, hip-hoppers, skateboarders. The popular crowd. Goths. Greasers. Computer geeks. What high school does not have them? Cliques sometimes overlap—jocks and cheerleaders are always part of the popular crowd, and in some schools skateboarders are also punks while in other schools maybe it is the hip-hoppers who skateboard. Cliques can also be known by different names—one school's "head-bangers" are a different school's "freaks." Yet no matter the over-lap, no matter what they are called, and no matter who is exclud-ed or included, high school cliques are not about to disappear or become any less important to teenagers. According to Bradford Brown, a professor at the University of Wisconsin-Madison who studies high school cliques, teens spend twice as much time with their peers as with their parents.

The *Gale Encyclopedia of Childhood and Adolescence* recognizes that "joining cliques, having the desire to join a particular clique, and being excluded from cliques are considered a normal part of adolescent development." Yet the same social scientists who say it is important for teens to have a group of friends also point out the dangers of overly exclusive cliques. They say cliques can be good, but are sometimes bad. Some cliques help teenagers find them-selves and form lasting friendships, but others are merely an excuse for members of the "in crowd" to humiliate non-members. And what about peer pressure—how are teenagers influenced by the behavior of their friends, whether for good or for bad?

Cliques Can Be Good

Cliques—or, at least, groups of friends with common interests—are central to the social life of teenagers. In fact, 36 percent of teens interviewed by the Gallup Youth Survey in 2001 said that their favorite way to spend an evening was "visiting with friends." That was the most popular choice (it has been the most popular since Gallup started asking the question in 1980), followed by watching television at 23 percent. But the two categories are not mutually exclusive, since in the poll the favorite activity of some teens appeared to be watching television with friends. One young man, for instance, said his ideal evening was "watching a DVD with my friends while chowing down on snacks." The same survey also found being with friends was more popular among girls than among boys (42 percent to 30 percent) and among older teens (47 percent of those aged 16 and 17, compared to 28 percent of 13- to 15-year olds).

Most social scientists who study teenage behavior agree that young people gain many benefits from spending time with friends. "Adolescents are beginning to form their own identity away from their parents," says Nancy Darling, a professor at Bard College who teaches courses on adolescent development. "Cliques aid in this new identity in that they provide a group of peers with common interests and values to identify with." Darling believes that peer groups provide teens with the emotional support they need to develop a personal identity and the social skills they use later in life.

Teens use those social skills even before they leave high school "My best friends were cool. We wore nice clothes, and we always got excited about the first day of class. This was when we could sport the newest look," recalls one young woman named Jennifer who was part of a study about teen life sponsored by Bard College. "Having these close friendships in my life gave me self-confidence to run for president of student council for the middle school. My friends and family really encouraged me to go for it, and so I did. The school had an assembly the day they were going to announce the winners for the officers for the student council that next year. Waiting was agony but hearing my name was one of the biggest thrills!"

Most teenagers, like Jennifer, believe they are popular. In a poll conducted by the Gallup Youth Survey in 2003, 42 percent of high school students described themselves as either "very popular" or "popular." Thirty-nine percent said they had "about average popularity." Psychologist Lawrence Steinberg, a nationally recognized authority on adolescent development, says that popular teens have the ability to see the needs of others and act on them with confidence, but without being conceited.

Eighteen percent of teens in the poll ranked themselves as "not so popular" or "not popular at all," but even the less-popular cliques can provide that much-needed sense of belonging, without the pressure of a popularity contest. "I don't really try to be popular. I used to try very hard, and it never really did me any good," one 16-year old girl told the Gallup Youth Survey. "Plus none of the popular people at my school were nice. Now I don't try at all, I actually avoid the popular kids, and I feel much better about myself. The friends I have are very nice, and I have enough that I'm not lonely." Added a 15-year-old boy, "I have a tendency to take up for the underdog or the new kid or the kid that is different. I don't care what that small group of the most popular kids (we call them 'preps') thinks. The preps are the ones that only hang out with kids

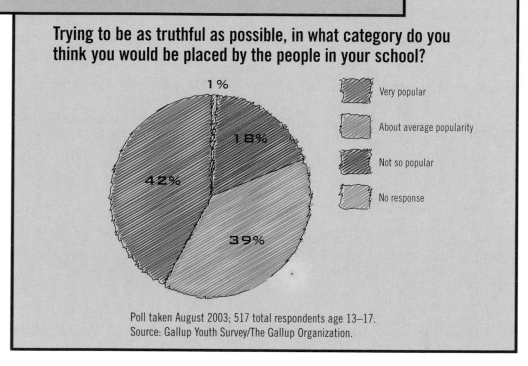

Trying to be as truthful as possible, in what category do you think you would be placed by the people in your school?

1 %

18%

42%

39%

Very popular

About average popularity

Not so popular

No response

Poll taken August 2003; 517 total respondents age 13–17.
Source: Gallup Youth Survey/The Gallup Organization.

who dress in high fashion, drive the newest cars, etc. I also don't like groups that try to follow a herd mentality. I have a good mind and I use it."

Cliques Can Be Bad

Those two teens that Gallup interviewed may not have been the most popular in their school, but at least they seemed to have found another group of friends with whom to hang out. So they were as popular as they chose to be. What happens when kids cannot fit in any group, who want to be popular but do not know how? Steinberg's research showed there are three types of unpopular adolescents. Some are aggressive and likely to get in fights, the typical "bullies." Others are withdrawn, too shy to make friends. Still others are a combination of aggressive and withdrawn — they can be hostile to other students and at the same time nervous in social situations. Whatever the case, despair about not fitting in anywhere is the common reaction.

"I hate coming to school," wrote a 13-year old girl on www.shine.com. "I'm getting F's and D's because I'm afraid of what people think of me. I cry because I'm always excluded. People talk about going to parties and other people's houses after school right in front of me, and I'm not invited." The website's editors responded with criticism of peer groups that demand conformity and show an attitude of superiority. "Cliques can exert harmful influences like hostile exclusion, interpersonal conflict, and bullying," they said. "Twenty percent of children are at the bottom of the social ladder. Often, the mental health of the bottom ten percent of these children is at risk due to loneliness or humiliation. Because they have no friends, they either develop a pattern of being passive and sad or they become aggressive. This is why exclusion from cliques has been cited as a reason for school violence." Dr. Steinberg, too, believes adolescents who suffer rejection show misconduct, self-centeredness, and aggression.

The 1999 shootings at Columbine High School, as well as other deadly school incidents, were carried out by teenagers who saw themselves as outcasts, needing to lash out at those who were more popular. Nearly one quarter of kids aged 13 to 17 surveyed by Gallup in 2003 answered "Yes" when asked if they feared for their physical safety in school. In another survey taken the same year, Gallup found that 37 percent of teens said they get teased or picked on at school, and that nearly a quarter (24 percent) had been in a physical fight during the past year. Thirty-one percent of teens who said they get teased or picked on at school also said they have been in a fight in the past year, compared with 20 percent of teens who do not get teased.

The survey also suggests that most of those who get in fights or are picked on tend to be teens with lower academic standing. Thirty-one percent of teens who say that they are "above average" or "near the top" of their class admit to getting teased or picked on, compared with 45 percent of teens who define their class standing as "average" or "below average." Just 16 percent of above-average kids said they have been in a fight in the past year, as did 36 percent of average or below-average kids. It may all go

This video footage shows Dylan Klebold and Eric Harris in the cafeteria of Columbine High School during their murderous 1999 rampage. The two boys felt like they were outcasts, and targeted popular students when they launched their attack.

back to cliques and popularity, Stan Davis, a social worker and author of *Schools Where Everyone Belongs: Practical Strategies for Reducing Bullying* told the Gallup Organization. "The more highly achieving students might have more social status in the school, more ability to deflect teasing through verbal responses, or might be kids who have more resources in their environments so the same teasing does not bother them," Davis said.

One problem, Bradford Brown says, is that often kids do not actually pick their group but are instead pulled into one almost despite themselves because of their personalities and interests. And if the group they find themselves in does not have high social standing, teens may try to gain acceptance from a more prestigious clique even if they have to reinvent themselves. "Many will change their whole personality to fit in or be with a certain group of people," explains a young person named Branden Aikey in an essay that was published on the website of Penn State University. "Some will change the way they dress or what they do to fit in. Also many will just go along with something even if they don't want to do it just so people will think they are one of them."

Rejecting Rejection

Some teens do not have to bother reinventing themselves, however. They smoothly and naturally glide into the clique of their choice as if they always belonged, and never experience peer rejection. They have what social scientists call "social competence," which Penn State professors Janet A. Welsh and Karen L. Bierman define as the "ability to establish and maintain high quality and mutually satisfying relationships and to avoid negative treatment or victimization from others." Socially competent teens, the two professors say, are friendly, self-confident, able to consider others' perspectives, and "engage readily in conversation."

But what about kids who do not have those skills? Some high schools have programs to help young people improve their social competence. They learn how to make friends and judge social situations so they can behave appropriately. Adolescents in this type of program, say researchers at Bard College, "are taught how to calm down and think before they react, decide what the problem is, figure out what their goal is, and to think about positive approaches toward reaching that goal. The intervention programs that have been designed to help teach youths how to make friends and gain the appropriate social skills needed have had a positive influence on helping rejected individuals form a social status."

Some teens avoid cliques because they want to define themselves as individuals, and don't feel that they need the approval of a group to be happy.

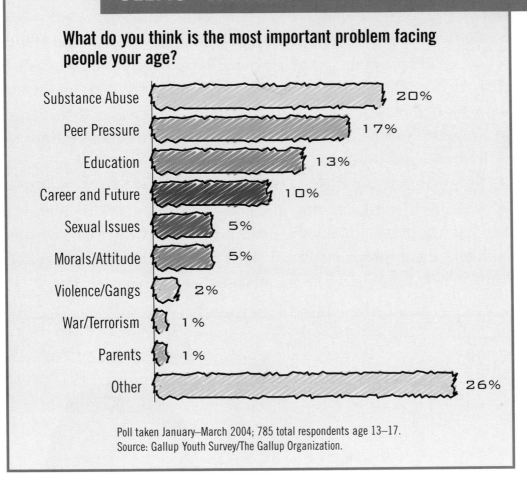

ISSUES WEIGHING ON TEENS' MINDS

What do you think is the most important problem facing people your age?

Substance Abuse	20%
Peer Pressure	17%
Education	13%
Career and Future	10%
Sexual Issues	5%
Morals/Attitude	5%
Violence/Gangs	2%
War/Terrorism	1%
Parents	1%
Other	26%

Poll taken January–March 2004; 785 total respondents age 13–17.
Source: Gallup Youth Survey/The Gallup Organization.

It is also true that some of the images people—not just teens—associate with cliques may not actually be what they seem. Traditionally, "jocks" are supposed to be the most popular boys, while among girls good looks is supposed to hold the key to popularity. Smart kids are often thought to be low on the social scale. But this idea of brawn and beauty over brains did not hold up in a Gallup Youth Survey conducted in 2000. Forty-two percent of girls aged 13 to 17 said they preferred to be the smartest person in the class, and only 18 percent said their ideal was to be the best looking. Among boys, being the captain of a major sports team was the preferred choice of 40 percent—yet almost as many, 36 percent, wanted to be the smartest. This suggests that being "the brain" in a high school does not by itself make anyone an outcast.

Peer Pressure

As long as there have been cliques, there has been peer pressure. A 2004 Gallup Youth Survey found 17 percent of 13- to 17-year-olds cited "peer pressure" as the most important problem teens face, the second most frequent answer behind "substance abuse" (20 percent), which can, of course, also be linked to peer pressure.

According to the *Gale Encyclopedia of Childhood and Adolescence*, "Peer pressure occurs when the individual experiences implicit or explicit persuasion, sometimes amounting to coercion, to adopt similar values, beliefs, and goals, or to participate in the same activities as those in the peer group." In *Coping with Peer Pressure*, Leslie Kaplan tried to define this in simpler terms. "Teens who act a certain way because they believe their friends expect that from them are feeling peer pressure," Kaplan wrote. Peer pressure can influence a young person's clothing, music, leisure-time activities, and choice of friends.

Having friends who exert pressure is not necessarily a bad thing, wrote Kaplan, because "peers offer independence from the family, acceptance, a sense of personal worth, support in times of confusion, models for appropriate conduct in a complex world, and social identity." Even the pressures themselves can be a force for good. Peer pressure "keeps youth participating in religious activities, going to 4-H meetings and playing on sports teams, even when they are not leaders," says Herbert G. Lingren, who studies families at the University of Nebraska. "It keeps adults going to religious services, serving on community committees and supporting worthwhile causes. The peer group is a source of affection, sympathy and understanding; a place for experimentation; and a supportive setting for achieving the two primary developmental tasks of adolescence." Lingren defines those tasks as "identity" (finding the answer to the question "who am I?") and "autonomy" (discovering a self that is dependent from parents).

That process of discovering the self apart from parents can in some cases mean that peer pressure is stronger than the influence of mom and dad. Lingren says that as adolescents find their new independence, "they begin to question adult standards and the need for parental guidance. They find it reassuring to turn for advice to friends who understand and sympathize—friends who are in the same position themselves." In weak families, that can be a positive. One study cited by the *Gale Encyclopedia of Childhood and Adolescence* found that, "Compared to others who started high school with the same grades, students whose families were not especially supportive but who spent time with an academically oriented peer group were successful."

Yet the encyclopedia also noted that the reverse was also true, because "those students whose families stressed academics but who spent time with peers whose orientation was not academic performed less well." And it is not only academics that can be heavily—and negatively—influenced by peers. The encyclopedia article also says, "Peer pressure similarly compels students of all ethnic backgrounds to engage in other at-risk behaviors such as cigarette smoking, truancy, drug use, sexual activity, fighting, theft, and daredevil stunts. Again, peer group values and attitudes influence, more strongly than do family values, the level of teenage alcohol use."

Substance Abuse

"I, myself, started drinking because my friends drank and they started drinking because their friends drank also," recalls one young man who went on to college to study the effects of peer pressure on teen drinking. "I didn't even like beer when I first started drinking. But I had to fit in so I drank." Leslie Kaplan's book cites one study that found nearly 80 percent of high school students interviewed said that they were pressured by peers to drink. Peer pressure affects drug use, too. A 1995 study published in the *American Journal on Addictions* found 84 percent of adolescents who tried drugs did so because of peer pressure. And the U.S. Surgeon General's office says that 10.6 million teens drink, about half the national population of high school juniors and seniors.

Gallup pollsters expanded that question in 2004 to include younger teenagers. The survey showed that 27 percent of teens between the ages of 13 and 17 admit to having imbibed an alcoholic beverage at some point in their lives. The frequency increased with

Peer pressure can exert a powerful influence—sometimes even stronger than parental authority. Some teens fall into alcohol and drug use simply because they seek the good opinion of their peers.

age: 37 percent of teens age 16 and 17 said they drank, compared to 20 percent of those aged 13 through 15. Overall, 74 percent said that alcohol abuse among teenagers is either a very serious (42 percent) or somewhat serious (32 percent) problem.

Another Gallup survey, from 2001, showed 54 percent of teens said it is very or fairly easy to get alcoholic beverages. Perhaps surprisingly, the 2001 Gallup Youth Survey also found young teenage girls, aged 13 to 15, are slightly more likely to admit to drinking than boys (5 percent and 3 percent respectively). But that changes the older teens get. Twenty-five percent of 16- to 17-year-old boys who drink say they "drink more than they think they should," compared to 14 percent of girls who admitted the same thing. Among all teens 13 to 17 years old, 12 percent of boys said they drink more than they think they should, compared to 9 percent of girls.

Ominously, in 2000 the Gallup Youth Survey found that 5 percent of young people admitted to having driven shortly after drinking alcohol, and 13 percent said they had been passengers in a vehicle driven by a drunk driver.

Gallup polls have focused not only on teen drinking, but also on teen drug use. One in five teenagers (20 percent) surveyed in 2004 said they had smoked marijuana. Gallup found that teenage boys are much more likely than teenage girls to say they have tried marijuana (28 percent compared with 12 percent), and that teens 16- to 17-years-old are nearly three times as likely as 13- to 15-years-olds to have tried the drug (32 percent to 12 percent.). One report by American Medical Association shows even higher drug use—it says more than half of all U.S. teenagers will have tried an illegal drug by the time they finish high school.

Teens are concerned about widespread drug use among their peers. Seventy-two percent of teens in the same poll characterized abuse of drugs such as marijuana and cocaine as either a "very serious" (52 percent) or "somewhat serious" (20 percent) problem for teens. In addition, 52 percent believed that the abuse of over-the-counter remedies such as cold medicine was a very serious (28 percent) or somewhat serious (25 percent) health issue among their peers.

Generation "No"?

Yet there is positive news. The Gallup Youth Survey has found that although some teens drink and take drugs, most young people believe drinking and taking drugs is a problem. What is more, the number of teens who abuse substances had been declining steadily. For 25 years, Gallup Youth Survey data have indicated that campaigns to deter teen drinking, smoking, and drug use have had an enormous impact on teen behavior, perhaps increasing peer pressure to stay away from harmful substances. Gallup has found that "the percentage of high school-age teens who smoke cigarettes, drink alcohol, and experiment with marijuana has declined dramatically over the last two decades—as much as 50 percent in each of the above categories."

For instance, in a 1979 Gallup Youth Survey, 24 percent of teens said they had smoked cigarettes during the previous seven days, while only 12 percent said the same in 2001. Polls show a significant drop in drinking, also. Alcohol use was at its highest in 1982, when 41 percent of kids admitted to drinking; in a 2004 survey just 27 percent said they drink. In addition, those young people who do drink are drinking less than they used to, the Gallup Youth Survey also found. The biggest drop, however, is in the number of teens who have tried marijuana: 41 percent said they had smoked pot in a 1979 Gallup survey, compared to 20 percent in 2004.

Chapter Six

Schools today are much more diverse than they were even 25 years ago. Most teens know people of different racial, cultural, or ethnic backgrounds, and studies have shown that young people today are much more tolerant than their parents.

Hanging With the Others

In Sioux Falls, South Dakota, high school students used the Internet to set up fights between U.S.-born and immigrant teenagers at a local park. In Salisbury, North Carolina, six white teens videotaped themselves throwing a cup of water and shouting racial insults at a black employee of a fast-food restaurant. Yet in Jackson, Mississippi—the site of a famous confrontation in 1961 between segregationists and civil rights marchers—black and white teenagers join together to work in food banks and other community service projects on Martin Luther King Day, in a program local organizers call "MLK: A day on, not a day off." And in Boca Raton, Florida, high school students volunteer to visit local grammar schools to teach the younger kids about tolerance between whites, blacks, Hispanics, Jews, and other ethnic and religious groups.

Teenagers, like most Americans, respond in different ways to the reality of an increasingly diverse society. The 2000 Census found that 81 percent of the U.S. population was white, 12.7 percent black, and 2.5 percent Asian; Hispanics (who can be of several different races) make up 12.6 percent of the population. By 2003 the Hispanic population was larger than the population of non-Hispanic blacks, 37 million to 36.2 million. And the Census projects that in 2050 barely more than one half of the population (50.1 percent) will be non-Hispanic white. Hispanics will then make up nearly a quarter of the American population, with blacks at 14.6 percent and Asians at 8 percent. This diversity can be seen in the student populations of many schools. For instance, in 2004 the *South Florida Sun-Sentinel* reported that in some counties near Miami students come from at least 150 countries and speak 104 different languages.

In a sense, the nation has gone through this before. The United States experienced similarly profound changes during the mass migrations of the 19th and early 20th century. Some 30 million immigrants arrived in the United States between the 1840s and the 1920s, mostly from Germany, Italy, Ireland, Russia, Poland, and the old Austro-Hungarian Empire. The Jewish immigrants among them encountered anti-Semitism. Those who were Roman Catholics were seen by nativists as agents of the Pope threatening to destroy the Protestant identity of colonial America. Most of the newcomers, regardless of their ethnicity or religion, found themselves facing the problems of **assimilation**, language, and poverty that many new immigrants of today face. This was true even of some people who had been in America from the earliest days. The contributions of African Americans to U.S. history, for example, were generally overlooked until after the **Civil Rights movement** of the 1950s and 1960s empowered black people by eliminating legal barriers to equality.

Yet even if the diversity of today has a historical echo, the changes can be difficult. "I am first generation *Hmong*, first in my family who was born an American citizen. Still, people always think that I'm a foreigner," a 16-year old named Madie wrote on the teen online magazine www.shine.com. "For example, when I was having trouble in one of my classes at school, I approached my professor for suggestions on how I could improve. He said, 'Oh, I thought that you couldn't understand me and didn't ask me questions because you were an international student.' I was so offended that he jumped to that conclusion because of my appearance."

Is that an example of how Americans are coping with the ethnic mix of the 21st century? Not necessarily. Several Gallup surveys suggest the people of the United States are coping fairly well. In 2001, 2002, and 2003 the Gallup Organization asked adults whether they thought relations between various ethnic groups were "very good, somewhat good, somewhat bad, or very bad." In all three years the leading answer was "somewhat good," a finding that remained consistent no matter which groups Gallup asked about and no matter the ethnicity of the respondents.

For example, in 2003 59 percent of whites and 50 percent of blacks agreed that relations between whites and blacks were "somewhat good," while only about a quarter of both whites and blacks said relations were "somewhat bad." Small minorities were at the opposite ends of optimism and pessimism. The most upbeat assessment? Eighty-four percent of Hispanics said relations between them and non-Hispanic whites were either "very good" (16 percent) or "somewhat good" (68 percent). The gloomiest? In the 2001 survey, 44 percent of non-Hispanic whites thought Hispanic-black relations were either "somewhat bad" (34 percent) or "very bad" (10 percent).

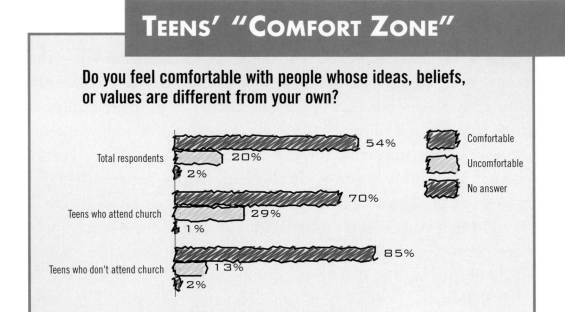

Do you feel comfortable with people whose ideas, beliefs, or values are different from your own?

Total respondents
- Comfortable 54%
- Uncomfortable 20%
- No answer 2%

Teens who attend church
- Comfortable 70%
- Uncomfortable 29%
- No answer 1%

Teens who don't attend church
- Comfortable 85%
- Uncomfortable 13%
- No answer 2%

Legend:
- Comfortable
- Uncomfortable
- No answer

Poll taken August 2003; 517 total respondents age 13–17.
Source: Gallup Youth Survey/The Gallup Organization.

Today's Open-Minded Teens

Those figures represent progress, given that a generation ago the United States was just leaving behind an era when blacks were forced to attend inferior schools and had to sit in the back of buses in some regions. But the surveys focused on adults. How do teens today feel about similar issues? The Gallup Youth Survey has found that U.S. teenagers are generally open-minded and tolerant when it comes to race or ethnicity. Recent surveys have found 80 percent of teens say they are offended by racial stereotypes in movies. The same number says it will make no difference to them whether their college roommate is black, white, Hispanic, or Asian. And 79 percent say they "feel comfortable being with people whose ideas, beliefs, and values are different from their own."

Teens questioned in the survey showed that feeling comfortable can be a matter of degree. Fifteen-year-old Josh Larsen, a high school sophomore from Omaha, Nebraska, says his comfort zone with people who have different ideas, beliefs, and values only goes so far. "As long as people don't try to press their views on me, I don't care," he said. "But if they're trying to make me be open to what they're talking about, without being open to what I'm talking about, it's annoying. If both of us are on the same field, then it's all right."

Teens can learn to become more tolerant, too. Lindsay, a high school junior from New Jersey, told the Gallup Youth Survey she had always felt "fairly comfortable" with people with different beliefs, but realized after spending a semester at the Island School in the Bahamas that she was not as open-minded as she thought. "My time at the Island School taught me to recognize my biases and where they come from," Lindsay said. Because of her experience there, she now feels "much more comfortable with other people who have different beliefs than I do. I give their opinions more thought and consideration."

The Gallup Youth Survey also found boys are more likely than girls to be at ease with "different" people: 83 percent of boys and 73 percent of girls said they are comfortable with people who have different views, values, and beliefs. And, perhaps surprisingly, the Gallup Youth Survey found that teens who regularly go to church or synagogue are less comfortable than teens who do not: 70 percent of churchgoing teens said they feel comfortable, compared to 85 percent of non-churchgoing teens. Churchgoers of all races, in fact, turned out to be the most ill at ease of all the demographic groups tested: 29 percent said they are uneasy with people whose ideas, values, and beliefs are different from theirs.

A Gallup report pondered the reasons why churchgoers seem less tolerant. "Social scientists have long explored the reasons why people who share similar attitudes, beliefs, and values tend to seek out people who are like themselves and develop fewer relationships with people who are different," said Gallup's experts. "This natural tendency, termed *values homophily*, could partially explain the differences among teens who go to church or synagogue and those who don't. Regular, frequent exposure to an organized belief structure, like a church or a synagogue, could explain why teens who attend them are more likely to exhibit values homophily."

Of course, what teenagers say about diversity is not the only thing that counts. Also important is how they have to act on those tolerant beliefs, given the opportunity. But according to a 2003 Gallup poll, most teens do not get many opportunities—at home or at school. Nationwide, 6 in 10 teens said their neighborhoods are all or mostly white, while 18 percent said their neighbors were all or mostly "minorities." Only 16 percent said they lived in racially mixed neighborhoods. The Gallup Youth Survey has found that U.S. schools also continue to be segregated, albeit less so than residential neighborhoods. Overall, 46 percent of teens said the students in their schools are all or mostly white and 18 percent said they are all or mostly non-white, compared to the less than one third (31 percent) who said they attended schools that were about half white and half non-white.

In other words, 78 percent of U.S. teens live in segregated neighborhoods and 64 percent attend segregated schools. Segregation persists even after laws forcing the separation of the races were declared unconstitutional in the 1950s and 1960s. Yet the Gallup Youth Survey shows that many teens do have a racially diverse group of friends. Sixty-seven percent of teenagers surveyed in 2003 said they are friendly with teens from other racial or

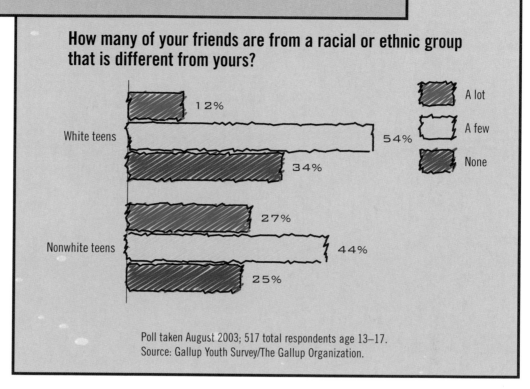

How many of your friends are from a racial or ethnic group that is different from yours?

White teens
- 12%
- 54%
- 34%

Nonwhite teens
- 27%
- 44%
- 25%

A lot
A few
None

Poll taken August 2003; 517 total respondents age 13–17.
Source: Gallup Youth Survey/The Gallup Organization.

ethnic groups (17 percent said they have "a lot" of racially diverse friends and 50 percent saying they have "a few"). Still, a sizeable 31 percent said all their friends belonged to the same ethnic or racial group.

But what does "being friends" mean? One 17-year old from Chicago told *Time* magazine he had more black than white friends, but clarified that he never visits black buddies who live in crime-plagued housing projects, and that the friendship amounts to "just talk in school." Pamela Perry, author of *Shades of White: White Kids and Racial Identities in High School* found that at one ethnically diverse school she studied white students tended to divide into cliques based predominantly on race, while at a mostly white school where race was less of an issue the cliques formed along other lines.

The teens with the most diverse circle of friends lived in the Western states, the Gallup Youth Survey found. That may be because they are also the most likely to both live in integrated neighborhoods and attend racially mixed schools where they find more opportunities to form friendships with teens of other ethnic groups. According to the 2000 Census, 26 percent of the population of Western states is Hispanic, making this one part of the country that has more minorities than any other region.

Another Gallup Youth Survey, taken in 2003, also found there are plenty of interracial friends in U.S. high schools. Sixty-seven percent of students surveyed said white students in their schools are friends with students of other backgrounds; 62 percent said the same thing about blacks; and 71 percent agreed Hispanics and

Asians have friends who come from different ethnic groups. Mayra Stafford, principal of Forest Hill High in West Palm Beach, Florida, sees that trend in her own school. "It's so mixed and so diverse, you'd be surprised the groupings you see. It's all one big mix," she said. Some of her students agreed. "You get to meet so many different people and learn about different languages and cultures," said Anneris Francisco, a senior whose parents are from the Dominican Republic. She added that even though she hears occasional racially disparaging insults, most students have a diverse group of friends.

Dating in Colors

Of course, "being friends" or "hanging out" takes on an entirely different meaning when gender is involved and it is boyfriends and girlfriends who are doing the hanging out. And when a couple happens to be *interracial* or *interethnic*, issues other than gender come into play—within the relationship as well as outside of it.

"I have always dated in and out of my race," says Heather, a New Jersey high school student of Irish and Norwegian ancestry. "I used to get teased a lot. Like my friends would make fun of me." Other teens hardly give it a second thought, like Cathleen Woods, a white high-school student in Fairfax County, Virginia, who is dating a Hispanic boy named David Negron. "For us, [dating] has nothing to do with color," Cathleen told the *Christian Science Monitor*. "You almost never think about it."

And when people do think about interracial dating, most think it is fine—even when it comes to whites and blacks, historically the most controversial mix in the United States. When the Gallup Organization asked adults in 2002 about black-white marriages, 65 percent of respondents said they approved. That was a significant increase over the 43 percent who approved of interracial marriage in 1983. But there seem to be differences between what blacks and whites think of the idea. When members of the two races were polled about racially mixed marriages in 1997, there was a gap of 16 percentage points between the two groups: 77 percent of blacks approved, compared to 61 percent of whites. Still, the gap is narrowing: In 1983 it stood at 33 points, with 71 percent of blacks saying they support black-white marriages compared to only 38 percent of whites.

There is also an age gap, because the young tend to be much more tolerant of interracial marriage, Gallup polls have shown. In the 2002 survey, a breakdown of the 65 percent of adult Americans who said they were fine with marriages between blacks and whites found that the approval of 18- to 29-year-olds stood at 86 percent, while only 30 percent of those aged 65 and older approved.

Teenagers have proven to be the most open-minded of any age group—when asked by the Gallup Youth Survey in 2001 whether they approve of black-white marriages, fully 91 percent of 13- to 17-year-olds answered yes. Teens have grown more tolerant as years go by: in 1977 only 52 percent approved of white-black marriages. And teens do not only approve of racially mixed marriages, they also approve of racially mixed dating. Fifty-five percent of white teenagers said they would be willing to date a black person, and 61 percent of blacks said they would date a white person, according to a 1997 Gallup Youth Survey.

Yet the willingness of so many teens to at least consider dating outside their race does not mean that black-white couples face no problems. Sometimes it is just stares and glares as an interracial couple walks down the street holding hands. Other times, things become more confrontational. As recently as 1994, the principal of a small school in Alabama threatened to cancel the prom if interracial couples attended. Experts say problems are more likely to crop up in small rural towns than in more racially mixed cities or suburbs, where residents are more used to ethnic diversity "People wouldn't blink an eye in Washington, D.C.," said Dr. David Weis, a professor at Bowling Green State University who teaches classes about race relations. "But in a small town, this is still big stuff."

Trouble can come from members of any race. One Bowling Green student who is black will long remember his feelings when going to the movies with his white girlfriend in her largely white home town. "I felt like every single person in the parking lot was looking at us, and every single person in the movie theater

Interracial relationships of a romantic nature are more widely accepted today than they were in the past. A 2001 survey found that 91 percent of teenagers approved of marriages between whites and blacks. In 1977, just 52 percent approved of interracial marriages.

watched the two of us walk to our seats," he said. For Heather, a white student at a suburban Virginia high school who dated a black teen named David, those stares and glares came from black girls. "They don't like a white girl taking their man, or something," she said.

Interethnic Dating

The growth of diverse ethnic groups is a reminder that in the United States issues of race and ethnicity are is no longer a question of white and black. Teens today know that when they get to be adults they will have all sorts of racial and ethnic marriage options, and they seem to like it. In a 2001 Gallup Youth Survey, 93 percent of teenagers approved of white-Asian marriages, and 94 percent approved of marriages between Hispanics and non-Hispanics. Five years earlier, the figures were 88 percent and 90 percent, respectively. (The Gallup Youth Survey did not ask about Asian or Hispanic mixed marriages before 1997).

Teens know, too, that they also have all sorts of interethnic dating options. A 1997 Gallup Youth Survey found that about 15 percent of white teens, 10 percent of black teens, and 25 percent of Hispanic teens have dated an Asian person. A third of white teens and 38 percent of black teens have dated a Hispanic person. And fully 82 percent of Hispanic teens have dated non-Hispanic white teens.

The same Gallup poll showed Hispanics are the most willing to date outside their ethnic group even if they have not done so. Part of that probably has to do with the fact that Hispanics are not actually a race in the sense that blacks and whites are a race. Some Hispanics are white, some are black, some are a combination of both, and some are neither—they are *mestizos*, the descendants of

Europeans and the indigenous people who lived in the Americas before the arrival of Christopher Columbus and other Europeans. As a result, those who are white or light-skinned do not attract much attention when they date non-Hispanic whites. For example, a female Bowling Green student who is white but not Hispanic and dated a Puerto Rican student from the same school said that they don't experience much prejudice when in public. "It probably helps that [her boyfriend] is so light-skinned," she said. "When I first met him, I didn't even know he was Puerto Rican."

Bowling Green professor Weis was not surprised that a Hispanic and non-Hispanic white couple would attract less "gawking eyes and disapproving looks" than a black and white couple. "Whites tend to regard Hispanics as more like whites than blacks," he said. On the other hand it may be just as true that a dark-skinned Hispanic is more easily accepted by blacks than a non-Hispanic white person. Maisha, an African-American high school student in New Jersey says that her mother had no problems with her dating a young Hispanic man. "When she met him, she was alright with it—as long as I don't bring home anybody white, I guess."

Still, couples that include one partner who is an immigrant—whether Hispanic, Asian, European, African, or whatever—may encounter cultural or linguistic barriers that U.S.-born couples, even racially mixed ones, never have to face. Christina, an Ecuadorean-American teen who lives in New Jersey, said that even though she was born in the United States, she prefers going out with Hispanic guys. "We have a similar language, they know how to dance," she says. "Once I did date a white male . . . he didn't have like the same characteristics, the same character. And I didn't feel as comfortable." For one Asian-American girl, the problem was the opposite. She

thought the white guy she once dated was too interested in Asian culture. "[He] played traditional music, visited Asia, etc.," she explained. "Then I began to wonder . . . did he see me as another element of his Asian-centric lifestyle? Certain comments he made, while flattering on the surface, started to seem more like the muses of a man mystified and inspired by all the 'exotic' beauties around him."

Yet another difficulty ethnically mixed couples may face has to do with religion. "My parents are kind of okay about [interracial dating]," said Sherle, a New Jersey teen whose family is Jewish and immigrated from Iran (formerly known as Persia). "It's not normal for a Persian girl to go out with a black person or any other person out of their race, but for me, I've talked to my parents about it and as long as they're Jewish, they're fine." Indeed, Gallup's 2001 survey found teens were more resistant to interreligious marriages than to interethnic or interracial marriages. Eighty-six percent approved of marriages between Jews and non-Jews, and 81 percent approved of Catholic/non-Catholic marriages. Those are high figures, but still lower than the 91 percent approval for black-white marriages, which in the past might have seemed more controversial.

Even with all these difficulties, however, the polling data makes clear that more than ever, teens in the United States are dating or at least thinking about dating persons from outside their own ethnic group. Does this foreshadow an era of increasing ethnic and religious tolerance as the nation grows ever more diverse? By far the leading reason teens give Gallup pollsters to explain why they would date someone of a different race is as old as humanity: they simply found the person attractive. Ironically, that ancient feeling of sexual attraction can also be called "new" when it comes to cross-ethnic sexual attraction in America. "In 1963, 59 percent of Americans agreed there should be laws banning marriage between blacks and whites," wrote Laura Bohn. "In a country where racial divisions still remain deep, the rise of interracial relationships is an enormously hopeful sign of progress in bridging barriers."

American teenagers continue to make progress in other relationships too, from getting along with their parents, to finding themselves through relationships with their friends and peers, to sharing joy and heartbreak with their romantic partners. The teen culture that was born a generation ago indeed makes today's teenagers a distinct group in American life, but despite worries about youthful complacency and materialism, it may well end up that their true distinction as adults will be to make their nation a better, more tolerant place to live.

Glossary

ASSIMILATION—the process whereby individuals or groups of differing ethnic heritage are absorbed into the dominant culture of a society.

BABY BOOMERS—nickname for the generation born between 1946 and 1964.

CIVIL RIGHTS MOVEMENT—the political and social efforts during the 1950s and 1960s to bring equal rights to blacks.

CLIQUE—an exclusive group of people held together by common interests, views, or purposes.

COHABITATION—living together as man and woman, but without being married.

COURTSHIP RITUAL—the instinctive actions many animals take to attract a mate.

CUSTODY—charge or control over a person exercised by a parent or adult in authority.

GENETIC CODE—information carried by living cells that determines physical appearance and may affect some patterns of behavior.

HMONG—an ethnic group with origins in Southeast Asia, principally the nation of Laos.

HORMONES—chemical substances manufactured by organs in the body that can affect behavior and physical appearance.

INSTINCTIVE—a natural, unplanned act resulting from inborn behavior.

INTERETHNIC—of, involving, or designed for members of different ethnicities.

INTERRACIAL—of, involving, or designed for members of different races.

NEURONS—brain cells that conduct and generate nerve impulses.

NUCLEAR FAMILY—a family group that consists only of father, mother, and children.

Glossary

SYNAPSES—pathways that connect neurons.

TRAUMATIC—causing a disordered mental state because of stress.

TWEENS—children at the age between childhood and adolescence, usually those 9 to 12 years of age.

VALUES HOMOPHILY—the tendency for people to seek relationships with others who share the same values, beliefs, and attitudes.

YOUTH CULTURE—a set of attitudes, values, and opinions shared by most young people and illustrated through popular music, literature, and other forms of expression.

Internet Resources

http://www.gallup.com

Visitors to the Internet site maintained by the Gallup Organization can find results of Gallup Youth Surveys as well as many other research projects undertaken by the national polling firm.

http://www.askheartbeat.com

An expert responds to letters from people looking for advice on dating issues, interracial and online relationships, cohabitation, sexuality, cheating, commitment, and other issues.

http://www.GlamourGals.org

Website for an organization that promotes understanding between teens and senior citizens.

http://www.shine.com

Online e-zine for young people, written by teenagers and covering many aspects of teen life.

http://www.teenadviceonline.org

Teen Advice Online (TAO) is a site where teens can seek support for their problems through a network of peers from around the globe. Volunteer counselors —some teens themselves—answer and offer advice on a variety of teen life issues.

http://www.teenoutreach.com

Teen Outreach is a site that features articles on teen life, a discussion board for teens to air out their issues, and long lists of categorized links to websites of interest to teenagers.

http://www.teenwire.com

This website provides information about sexuality and relationship issues.

Internet Resources

http://www.wholefamily.com

The WholeFamily Community website provides resources and advice for people (teens, parents, couples, or seniors) who want to build strong, healthy, loving relationships. The site features a team of experts and professionals that offer real life solutions to some of the toughest challenges that families face today.

http://www.youthcomm.com

A site that features articles written by aspiring teen journalists covering relationships with family, peers, and dating partners.

Further Reading

Carter-Scott, Chérie. *If High School is a Game, Here's How to Break the Rules: A Cutting Edge Guide To Becoming Yourself*. New York: Delacorte Press, 2001.

Covey, Sean. *The Seven Habits of Highly Effective Teens*. New York: Simon & Schuster, 1998.

Daldry, Jeremy. *The Teenage Guy's Survival Guide*. Boston: Megan Tingley Publishing, 1999.

Fuller, Natalie. *Promise You Won't Freak Out: A Teenager Tells Her Mother the Truth About Boys, Booze, Body Piercing, and Other Touchy Topics (and Mom Responds)*. New York: Berkley Publishing Group, 2004.

Kaplan, Leslie. *Coping with Peer Pressure*. New York: Rosen Publishing Group, 1996.

Kirberger, Kimberly. *Teen Love: On Relationships*. Deerfield Beach, Fla.: HCI Teens, 1999.

Mayall, Beth. *Get Over It! How to Survive Breakups, Back-Stabbing Friends, and Bad Haircuts*. New York: Scholastic, 2000.

Nikkah, John. *Our Boys Speak: Adolescent Boys Write About Their Inner Lives*. New York: St. Martin's Press, 2000.

Wiseman, Rosalie. *Queen Bees and Wannabes: Helping Your Daughter Survive Cliques, Gossip, Boyfriends, and Other Realities of Adolescence*. Three Rivers Press, 2003.

Index

Numbers in **bold italic** refer to captions and graphs.

Index

Index

Index

Picture Credits

Contributors

GEORGE GALLUP JR. is chairman of The George H. Gallup International Institute (sponsored by The Gallup International Research and Education Center, or GIREC) and is a senior scientist and member of the GIREC council. Mr. Gallup serves on many boards in the area of health, education, and religion.

Mr. Gallup is recognized internationally for his research and study on youth, health, religion, and urban problems. He has written numerous books including *My Kids On Drugs?* with Art Linkletter (Standard, 1981), *The Great American Success Story* with Alec Gallup and William Proctor (Dow Jones-Irwin, 1986), *Growing Up Scared in America* with Wendy Plump (Morehouse, 1995), *Surveying the Religious Landscape: Trends in U.S. Beliefs* with D. Michael Lindsay (Morehouse, 1999), and *The Next American Spirituality* with Timothy Jones (Chariot Victor Publishing, 1999).

Mr. Gallup received his BA degree from the Princeton University Department of Religion in 1954, and holds seven honorary degrees. He has received many awards, including the Charles E. Wilson Award in 1994, the Judge Issacs Lifetime Achievement Award in 1996, and the Bethune-DuBois Institute Award in 2000. Mr. Gallup lives near Princeton, New Jersey, with his wife, Kingsley. They have three grown children.

THE GALLUP YOUTH SURVEY was founded in 1977 by Dr. George Gallup to provide ongoing information on the opinions, beliefs and activities of America's high school students and to help society meet its responsibility to youth. The topics examined by the Gallup Youth Survey have covered a wide range—from abortion to zoology. From its founding through the year 2001, the Gallup Youth Survey sent more than 1,200 weekly reports to the Associated Press, to be distributed to newspapers around the nation. Since January 2002, Gallup Youth Survey reports have been made available on a weekly basis through the Gallup Tuesday Briefing.

ROGER E. HERNÁNDEZ is a nationally syndicated columnist and the author of *Cubans in America* (Kensington Publishing, 2002) as well as several books for Mason Crest Publishers. He teaches journalism and English composition at the New Jersey Institute of Technology in Newark, where is writer-in-residence, and at Rutgers University. He lives with his family in New Jersey.